LAP

A HIGH SIERRA CHRISTMAS
An Untold Tale of Jeremiah Johnson

Latest Holiday Edition
July 2010

A bit of fiction and reality from award winning author
Mark Stephen Taylor

A HIGH SIERRA CHRISTMAS
An Untold Tale of Jeremiah Johnson
by Mark Stephen Taylor
(Latest Holiday Edition, July 2010)

Printed in the United States of America

ISBN 1449594972
EAN-13 is 9781449594978

An Italicized *word* or group of *italicized words* in the narrative indicate an emphasis on that/those particular word(s).

There are places in this story where the west reads "the West." A capital 'W' is simply the author's style, and indicates an emphasis on the famous haunts of the mountain men, cowboys and Indians of the late 1850's to early 1900's.

Superscripts (i.e.[1]) found in the text indicate that further information is available in the *References and Notes* section at the back of this book, where that information is listed in numerical order, by chapter.

The author designs any graphics in this book. Photos in this book were taken by the author, and by Dan Campbell of Searcy Arkansas (used by permission), and remain the property of the author. Photos by Dan Campbell are so indicated.

Any portion of this book may be reproduced for teaching and classroom use. All teachable information in this book is a product of the study, research, notes and personal experiences of the author. The story is fictional, but all Biblical teachings woven into the context of the story are true, and are indicated in the *References and Notes* section in the back of this book. Any statements (excluding Biblical statements) found within this writing, as well as events portrayed in this writing, that are similar to other fiction or non-fiction publications, with the exception of those which adhere to the Johnson legend, are purely coincidental.

Hikingthetrailoftruth.com productions.
MSTaylor Productions, Lone Wolf Limited,
hikemark@hotmail.com

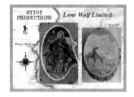

For The Reader
Other Books Available from this Author

Hiking the Trail of Truth is an award-winning autobiography, which has received excellent reviews. The desire to know God is universal—we want to understand our connection. Gear up to explore a diversity of eye-opening trails throughout the American southwest in the company of the author. You will climb Mt. Whitney as well, highest peak in the contiguous USA. If you've got what it takes to endure this most enlightening and illuminating journey of discovery, it will indeed be *well* worth your time.

($13.95, 298 pages, paperback)

From the Lone Wolf Limited Mystery Series comes the first two installments...**The Sun, The Glass, and The Leaning Rock;** The Secret of the Lost Dutchman's Gold, is a daring tale of high adventure. The story opens in the year 1984, but centers on the 1924 discovery of the 'Lost Dutchman's mine' in Arizona, the inevitable misfortune of its discoverer, and the strange fate of the loot itself. A treasure map, an unusual necklace, and a simple nursery rhyme set the stage for double murder, betrayal, kidnapping, and unrelenting drama in this tale of the high desert!

($11.95, 194 pages, paperback)

The Secret of Monument Valley, The Trail of the Anasazi, resolves the age-old mystery regarding the 1450 AD disappearance of the Anasazi people from their strongholds in the American southwest. Based on actual accounts from Native American residents of the Navajo Nation, award-winning author Mark Stephen Taylor thrusts his characters into the heart of this most interesting controversy. What they must endure is indeed most shocking. What they will find is most profoundly enlightening!

($11.49, 162 pages, paperback)

For Body, Mind, and Spirit: *Hiking Life's Difficult Trails* is an arduous challenge. These particular journeys are better suited to hikers who have learned to live with remorse, earned through a broad diversity of loss, pain and suffering. There are those who have what it takes to endure these journeys, and there are those who do not. Yet, being among the rare breed who have what it takes has only one requirement—humility.

We all fail in one way or another each day. Admit it or not, we just can't seem to attain perfection. We usually blame God for our inability to live as we should, but then praise Him when He allows things to get a little better. We just can't seem to find a way to be content in our circumstances, and be thankful for both the good ones and the bad ones. The bottom line is, we actually have some profound misunderstandings—about life, about circumstances, and about God Himself. Hiking is indeed great therapy and a time for learning. So, what are you waiting for? C'mon along—lets do it!

(\$8.95, 112 pages, paperback)

The ***High Country Hikers Edition*** of *Hiking Life's Difficult Trails* contains the same, life-changing information as the original edition (above), yet also adds a short but uniquely organized 7-day daily devotional at the end of the book, arranged by the author himself. Its purpose is to teach and inspire explicitly those who are partial to the more glorious treks of the high mountains (the 'high lonesome').

(\$9.95, 132 pages paperback)

* Any of these aforementioned books can be ordered from your local retailer, purchased on the internet, or purchased via the author's website, hikingthetrailoftruth.com.

A HIGH SIERRA CHRISTMAS
An Untold Tale of Jeremiah Johnson
Table of Contents

Title Page…….……………………………………....1
Copyright Page…………………………………....2
For the Reader……………………………..……4
Table of Contents………………………………...6
Dedications………...…………………….….……7
A Real Cast of Characters……………………...…9

From the Author……...…….………………….....11

Chapter 1…*The Family Arrives*…………………15
Chapter 2…*The Two Strangers*……………….…29
Chapter 3…*Robbery at Big Pine*…………………43
Chapter 4…*Into the High Country*………………57
Chapter 5…*The Outlaws!*…………………..………71
Chapter 6…*A Christmas Miracle*………………...85
Chapter 7…*The Wisdom of the Mountain Man*…..99
Chapter 8…*Truly His Brother's Keeper*………......117
Chapter 9…*A High Sierra Christmas*…………..133
Epilogue……………………………………..…...143

References and Notes……….……………….…...155

Mr. Phil Henry and son

Dedications

This book is first of all dedicated to *Phil Henry* (pictured above). Phildo is one of my best friends (and former partners in law enforcement), whom I camped and explored with several times over the years throughout the wilderness areas of southern California. We had a variety of adventures together, some of which happen to have been the most rewarding and vividly memorable of my entire life.

Phil and I spent time in some very inspiring locations during the late 1980's and early 1990's, one of which areas make up the entire background for this story. The characters in this tale of the High Sierra have all originated from family and friends, in honor of those family and friends; therefore, this work becomes a most special tribute to those folks. Phil Henry plays a major part in this enlightening adventure.

A High Sierra Christmas is also dedicated to each of the following beloved persons (cast of characters), who play a part in the story in one way or another...

7

In honor and in memory of Pauline Evelyn Boley Taylor
1918-1959

A Real Cast of Characters
In order of mention or appearance…

Note: The real characters (column 2) in this story play fictional parts (column 1) in the story. However, in a few cases, the fictional characters do not reflect the admirable qualities of the real life characters. In other words, the story is all in fun, and no offense is meant to any of these most wonderful friends and family, who play a part in this remarkable tale of the West.

Narrator, Mitchell J. Johnson	Mitchell S. Taylor
Gideon Johnson	Mark S Taylor
Jeremiah Johnson	Michael S Taylor
Marc Johnson	Marc Taylor
Carrie Johnson	Carrie Taylor
Hannah Johnson	Hannah Taylor
Bryce Perez	Bryce Rowland
Cael Perez	Cael Rowland
Riley Perez	Riley Virginia Taylor
Mikey Perez	Mike Taylor Jr.
Joseph Perez	Joseph Taylor
John Windwalker	Phil Henry
Railroad Ron	Ron Friend
Ed Shay	Ed Ostashay
Mr. David Perez	David Perez
Sheri (Mrs.) Perez	Sheri Perez
Sheriff Ken Petty	Ken Petty
Armando Valencia	Armando Valencia
Riccardo San Dona	Rick Sandona
White Eyes Chapman	Charles Chapman
Harry Brown	Harry D. Brown
US Marshal, Lil' Dave Swearengin	Dave Swearengin

9

Ryan Running Horse.........................Ryan Taylor
Cameron White Eagle.....................Cameron Taylor
Mason Kicking Bird........................Mason Taylor
US Deputy Marshal, "Doc" Gilmore....Steve Gilmore
Georgina Swearengin......................Georgina Swearengin
Sean Swearengin............................Sean Smith
Taylor Swearengin..........................Taylor Perez
Pauline Johnson.............................Pauline Evelyn Taylor
Running Horse (John Perez)..............Rod Florea

We're all travelers in this world, from the sweet grass to the packin' house; from birth until death, we travel between the eternities...

Author Unknown

10

Mark Stephen Taylor

From the Author

If you've read my very first publication, *Hiking the Trail of Truth, Knowing God through His Creation*, then you are well aware of what I enjoy writing about the most. But, I've always had the desire to write a fictional story of the West—a tale of the men, women and children, who lived in the American West during the historical period known as 'the late 1850's to the early 1900's.' These were the final days of glory for the Native American's of the West, the mountain men of the Rockies, and the history making explorers of the High Sierra Nevada.

Why would a former California police officer, educated in criminal psychology, geology, and now a Biblical teacher and counselor—why would he want to write a fictional story about the American West? First of all, Jesus left us a fine example— He was a storyteller. That's how He reached out to folks. Secondly, I grew up in the late '40's and early '50's, addicted to the radio and later televised stories of the Lone Ranger, Roy Rodgers, Zorro, Robin Hood, and Davy Crockett.

11

I spent much of my life wanting to be a combination of these folks—an adventurous, pure hearted defender of the realm. I wanted my realm to be the American West, and so it has become. If I combine the above listed gentlemen into a mix, stir it real good, and then drop that blend into the high, Sierra Nevada; I end up with a song of the West—a mountain man—honest, strong, adventurous, dependent upon the wilderness and a friend to its inhabitants.

Of course, it is man's nature to not do what is right—no one is pure in heart.[1] However, a Godly man, who knows what the Scriptures teach, is apt to fare much better while living out his dreams in the American West. So, I wanted to write about such a man (I chose a legendary character), about his family, his relatives, his friends, his neighbors, his love of the wilderness, and weave it all together into an enlightening tale of the Christmas Season (my favorite holiday).

I also wanted to present some Biblical teachings, related to the story, which would help readers to understand some of the deeper mysteries surrounding God and the attitudes of men. This is what Jesus did on a full time basis. Thirdly, I wanted to present an adventurous story, a family story, a meaningful story, a thought-provoking story, an educational story, and a non-traditional tale of the American West—narrated in the Old West style.

As a result of mixing all of these ingredients together (preceding paragraphs), I have been allowed to produce, *A High Sierra Christmas*. It's a story for all audiences; Christian and non-Christian alike, young and old alike. You can get together with your children, your grandchildren, your friends and your neighbors, your parents, and even your grandparents, if they're still kickin', and gather yourselves in front of the Holiday fire for a delightful reading of this tale.

I suppose that the reading/telling of this story can be considered entertainment, but I believe you will find it to be *much more* than that. If you want to add some flavor to the story, go ahead and read it to yourself beforehand, and then perhaps you can have the foreknowledge on how to portray the various voices (and perhaps imitate the facial/physical expressions) of the characters involved in the story, as you read it aloud to your audience. After all, a story truly only comes to life when you bring it to life—when you step into it and make yourself a part of it.

Stories are the essence of life. The universe began with the story of creation, and each of us plays a part in that story, which individual parts themselves have become the stories within the story. We're going to enter into the lives of a few of those individual parts and share a Christmas Season with them. *Happy Holidays* to you and yours as well (no matter what time of year it is)!

Are you ready? Then let's have some fun—let's take off our hiking boots for a brief time, put on our cowboy boots, climb aboard a horse, and head into the majesty of the High Sierras. It's there where we can ride into the scenery (a picture at the beginning of each chapter) and join up with the characters in this tale and actually become a part of their story —a part of *A High Sierra Christmas*…

Looking down at Mirror Lake on the Mt. Whitney Trail

The Family Arrives
Chapter 1

Howdy. My name's Mitchell J. Johnson—grandson to one Gideon Johnson. 'Mitch' is what I go by. You've probably never heard of either one of us, and that don't really matter none. But I reckon you *have* heard of my granddad's brother— Jeremiah Johnson? Lot's of stories 'bout him and his kind— mountain men. A rare breed. By the way, that's my middle name—Jeremiah.

Around the mid-1800's, Jeremiah Johnson left home at a young age, joined a war, then mustered out and went west, into the Rockies. Most of you know that story. It's been told time and again. There are several versions of it—some fact—some legends—most hearsay. Some newspaper folks say that when legend becomes fact, you best print the legend—sells more papers. I'd have to disagree with 'em in this case. The real facts behind Jeremiah Johnson's story are better than any ol' legend.

Some folks think Indians killed him off—Crow. Others say he's still wanderin' up in them mountains—the high and mighty lonesome. Well, they're both wrong. Fact is, after a time, Jeremiah left the Rockies, drifted into Canada for a spell, then come back south and took up root in the High Sierra Nevada, near the Whitney region, in central California.[1] He found gold there, and the man took to ranchin'.

I'd say most all of what I'm about to tell you is true, and the rest? Well, the rest is the West. Of course, I didn't believe it either when my Dad first told me this story—not right off. I'm no dang fool, and Dad knew not to take me for one. But, later on, I did believe him—he showed me some letters to prove it. I didn't read most of the letters 'till after Dad was gone, though —I regret that.

15

Now, I've told my own share of stories, and I heard a lot too, but this one my Dad told me—well—I've never heard the like. Wherever they get to, all *good* stories begin and end in the same place, and that's in the heart of a man—or a woman. Words from the heart are what they live by—if not, then there was somethin' seriously wrong with their upbringin'. And so, with the letters my Dad had to back up this story, I figured I'd come forward and set the record straight for ya'll.

Like I said, Dad's gone now—lost him in '63, and I'm the only one alive who knows this whole story. I figured you might want to know too—about another side of the mountain man, Jeremiah Johnson—and hear an enlightenin' tale as well—actually, more than enlightenin'! He warn't crazy, and he didn't eat no Injun's livers. In fact, he let go of his revenge and made peace with the Crow before he even left the Rockies.

Legends say he was a man who kept to himself—for the most part—a man who made his own peace with God and went on livin'. Believe it or not he knew a lot more about God than the legends might let on. He read his Bible, and he roamed God's mountains—them finely sculptured Rockies, and later, the High Sierra Nevada, which, myself, I believe to be the finest of God's artwork. I swear—they're magnificent!

Locals say he died up there in the Sierras, but his good friend, a Crow Indian, name of John Windwalker, never told nobody where he was buried. Myself, I think he lives on—at least in my heart anyway. Maybe it's the spirit of this story itself that lives on. Anyway, as I said, I'm gonna' set everything straight—and I got my reasons. So, without no further ado, here's the High Sierra tale as it was told to me:

I'm his kin, his grandnephew. As a boy I remember my grandfather, Jeremiah's brother, Gideon, and as I grew up I listened to my father, Marc Johnson, who was actually there—right there where this story took place. He told me this story that I'm about to tell you, and like I said, backed it up with

16

some letters, which I still have. To this day it's by far the best Christmas story I ever heard—except for the original one, of course—and I've been around a long time.

One Christmas season, many years ago—around 1890, I believe—Jeremiah Johnson had invited his two nieces and his only nephew to come out West for a long, overdue visit. The man at that time lived near a town called Big Pine, which is still there, at the foot of California's High Sierras—the eastern range. The three youngsters arrived by railroad, all the way from the Ohio country. These three were my Dad and his sisters—my aunt Carrie and my aunt Hannah.

Meetin' 'em, with great joy I might add, at the train station in the nearby town of Independence, Jeremiah helped 'em aboard his horse drawn wagon, stowed their luggage, and a short time later the four of 'em started out together on a twenty mile or so journey back toward Big Pine—Jeremiah had a spread just north of town—a good sized spread, too.

It was a warm day along that old, windin' road; a brilliant sun shinin' above the tall, mountain peaks, and most of the snow was on the melt at the lower elevations that they were passin' through. You could still see the beauty of it higher on up, though. It was the first time them youngsters ever set eyes on the lofty, white granite of the Sierras, and they never forgot about it—became a part of 'em after that...

"Are we going do some hiking, Uncle Jeremiah?" Carrie, the elder of the two sisters asked. The younger sister, Hannah, echoed that question and nodded her head in anticipation. They were seated just behind Jeremiah in the bed of the wagon. Marc (my Dad) rode shotgun, without a gun of course. He was just ten years old at the time. Aunt Carrie was fifteen—well educated I might add, and my aunt Hannah, she had just turned nine. And she was a pistol, that's for sure!

"We heard you guided folks all over these big mountains—is that true, Uncle Jeremiah?"

The man pulled on the reins while speakin' gently to his team of horses, bringin' the wagon slowly to a halt.

"I've been around." He looked kindly at his kin; the delight of their questions indeed brought warmth to his heart—he had never seen 'em before. He was mighty content that they were there with him. They were family—and that had become real important to him at the time.

"I can tell you some real good stories," he spoke softly, gently shakin' the reins to start them horses movin' again. "Last Christmas I got chased by a bear—a big, mean grizzly bear. He came running after me in the dark and was right on my heels, until, well—want to hear the whole story?"

The girls were filled with both excitement and joy at his suggestion. It was a mite hard for them to contain themselves.

"Tell us now," Carrie encouraged. "Yeah, tell us now, Uncle Jeremiah," Hannah echoed. She was one who echoed her sister most of the time. I suppose Carrie was just about the most important person in her life. She was for sure a fine role model.

My Dad was silent beside Jeremiah, his eyes roamin' the landscape. It was a much better view—sittin' atop that open wagon seat, than lookin' out the window of a movin' train—all boxed in and not even able to smell the air? The rugged, majestic peaks of the High Sierra are a mite captivatin', especially when you see 'em for the very first time from the open country down below 'em, and when twenty foot or more of white snow is sittin' on top of 'em. The sights and scents of the Sierra reach down inside you like no other—right down to the bone and marrow.

My Dad had Jeremiah's blood in him, that's for sure. Deep down he just wanted to jump out of that wagon and get to explorin' them high lonesome—climbin' the rocks and such.

18

He wanted to reach out and touch the high, icy pine and wade through the deep snow. He wanted to climb up as high as he could, just to look back down and see how far he'd come. He wanted to take a deep breath of all that beauty, put his hands on the white granite, soak in its grandeur and just keep wanderin' around on it. What young boy wouldn't?

Jeremiah tilted back his hat and relaxed somewhat on the reins as he begun to tell his story. The trio was all ears.

"Well, last Christmas I was decorating the tree inside the cabin—nice little blue spruce pine that I brought down from the mountain—only a few of them in this part of the country. They grow in Colorado mostly. I had some popcorn and a little tinsel, some candles too, and the whole thing was turning out quite fine.

"It was Christmas Eve, and I wasn't expecting anybody. I had my hands full of decorations, when I heard someone knocking at the front door. Well, I put the decorations down on the table and walked on over to the door to see who was there. When I opened the door, there stood Bryce Perez, a young boy who lives down the lane a bit with his folks. He has a younger brother, Cael, who usually tags along with him, but he was all by himself this time. He had a cookie tin in his hands, and offered it to me.

"He said, 'My ma made you some fudge and cookies, Mr. Johnson. She said you wouldn't be havin' any visitors this year, and she wanted to know if you could come down for breakfast tomorrow? She's makin' that sausage and egg casserole—always makes it this time of year. It's real good, Mr. Johnson—will you come?'

"Well, I reached out and took the tin out of the boy's hands and thanked him for it. 'Sure,' I said, 'I'll come over at first light. Is that okay?'

"'That's good,' he said. Then he said, 'I've got a project I'm workin' on—maybe you could help me with it?'

19

"'What's that?' I asked him. 'I'm buildin' a house for my turtle,' he answered. 'I have a little pen I made him out of rock, out back in the field, but it's been snowin' somethin' awful, and he don't have no place to keep warm. He don't like to stay in the house 'cause my dog keeps snappin' at him.

"'He can't get his head out of his shell much. Ol' Sam, my dog, just ain't made friends with him yet—he's part wolf. My cousins, Riley Virginia, Mikey, and Joseph, are over for the holidays, and they keep Ol' Sam riled up anyway. I never see'd such a racket!'

"I then told the boy that I could help him build his turtle house. I told him I could bring my tools along in the morning, and some old pieces of wood that I had out back. I told him that particular wood would make a fine house, as it was oak. Well, his eyes lit up like the candles on that Christmas tree.

"'I can stay a spell and help you with the tree,' he said. I told him that sounded fine. 'Come on in where it's warm,' I said to him. He stepped inside, grinnin' like a possum, and shut the door behind him. I asked him where his brother was and he told me that Cael was helping his ma with some Christmas baking. Said he had a sweet tooth, and was a mite busy sampling cookies—didn't want to come along.

"We soon got to working on decorating the tree, and kind of lost track of time. Before I knew it, it was pitch dark outside. I couldn't let that boy walk home in the dark by himself. Fact is, we'd seen a bear in the area about a week before, and most folks were staying inside at night. It was a big ol' grizz.

"They like to prowl around at night and hunt for food. They won't usually bother you if you're moving around in their territory, but if you're totin' any food, they'll chase you for sure! I use to wrap meat in burlap when I came off a hunt, but it didn't matter. Bears can smell food better than a mile off. I had to sleep with one eye open many a' time at my campsite.

20

You have to keep wood on the fire, that's sure. They don't like to come near fire."

With the town of Independence behind and fadin' out of sight, Jeremiah and the young'uns soon come to the fork of the Big Pine cut off. At this point the ol' road leveled off somewhat, and then begun its wind along Lone Pine creek, through the heavier groves of pine—them lofty ones that sprout cones near a foot tall and half as wide. There was a lot of water runnin' off the mountains that year too—run down 'em all year long. The roar of all that water in the creek was both an enjoyable sight and sound to the young trio.

An eagle soared majestically overhead, just as they cleared the rough water below Horseshoe Falls. Jeremiah pointed him out to the youngsters. They were in no small way captivated by the eagle's grace. He floated just above 'em for quite some time, ridin' them currents due north of Mt. Whitney. An eagle in flight is a fine thing to see. An eagle's way is mighty bold— hard to comprehend.

"That eagle's headed for the Needles," Jeremiah said. "Take me near two days to ride up there and—well, I believe he's there already." Jeremiah then looked over at the youngsters. "A couple hours from here and we'll be at the cabin.

"Anyway, as I was saying, thinking there might be a grizz out there, I wouldn't let the boy walk home by himself in the dark. So, I got my coat on and helped him with his, and we went on out into the night, headed down the lane toward the Perez place. The place wasn't far off, but the snow was getting a little heavy and the clouds were moving in low—foggier by the minute. It was then that we heard the bear. He was growling and he was close!"

"Wow," Carrie breathed.

"Wow," Hannah echoed.

Carrie reached forward and put her hand upon her uncle's arm, wringin' the sleeve of his jacket in her grip. "What happened, Uncle Jeremiah—mercy me! What did you do?"

"Fortunately we could still see the road in the fog, and so we ran. I figure it's better to stand still when a bear is close, but the boy took off running and I had to stay on his heels! I felt sort of responsible for that little sh—that little *man* that night! He could run too, but I finally caught up with him and grabbed his hand and ran alongside him. I looked down at his little face and he was scared, that's for sure—poor kid."

Suddenly Jeremiah pulled up on the reins of the horses, bringing the wagon to a halt. He pointed up the road, alerting the trio; "Elk up ahead there—crossing the road—see them? Big ones!"

Indeed they were huge. Mountain elk stand as tall or taller than most men. They are a sight to behold in the wild. When you see 'em for the first time you ain't never gonna' forget it. They stand with their heads proud, and hearin' 'em call out to one another is quite an experience.

"There's two bucks!" Carrie breathed. "I can see their horns."

"Are they horns or antlers, Uncle Jeremiah?" It was Hannah who posed the question. She echoed her sister's words most of the time, as I said before, but when she didn't and posed her own question, you knew there was somethin' a mite important on her young mind. It was best to answer her back. She was a mite shy and needed to be reminded now and again that her words were significant to a conversation. She would always tend to talk more when you could give her that feelin'.

"We'll, they're both, Hannah. They're basically horns, but that particular type or style of horn *is* known as an antler. An antler is just a branched or forked horn. Several different kinds of animals have them. They're called a 'rack' by the hunters, and they are a wonder—something nature gives them animals for protection as well as beauty."

"We've been studying animals in school, Uncle Jeremiah," Carrie said. "I'm in the ninth grade now—Hannah's only in third grade, so she hasn't learned a lot about the animals yet, but she's real curious about them. The class I have is called *science*. It's a new class at the school, and some of the things my teacher talks about are really weird.

"She talks about us coming from monkeys or something—*evolution* is the word she uses. We all laugh at some of the things the she says. She gets so mad at us for laughing! But, it is kind of stupid—coming from monkeys and stuff, don't you think so, Uncle Jeremiah?"

"That is pretty silly, Carrie. I swear—I don't know what this world is coming to. That's why I like it up here in the high country. I don't pay much attention to what goes on down in town—never been much for town dwellin', nor the things they fuss about down there. Town folk's seem a bit—" Jeremiah's eyes hit on the elk once again "—a bit cut off from reality.

"Look! There's three bucks now, and five doe. Heading up for higher ground, I guess. There's a nice green meadow up above—plenty of food for those critters to eat. No hunters up there this time of year. I'm sure the deer and elk are comfortable with that."

He shook the reins once again and the horses pulled onward. The creek was below 'em now, and the taller, snow-covered pines dominated the horizon. Quite a breathtakin' sight for those young newcomers, who were bent on takin' it all in.

"What happened with the bear, Uncle Jeremiah?" Carrie asked, as she and Hannah watched the elk move on until they was dang near out of sight.

"Well, we made it to the boy's house. I don't think the bear was actually stalking us, but we could hear him out there. The fog was so thick that we couldn't see forty feet from the Perez place. They asked me to stay all night there, but I had to get back. I'd left those candles burning on the Christmas tree, and I was a little worried that something might catch fire in the cabin —wind was stirring a little bit.

"I told them all I'd be back for that breakfast, after which I'd help the boy with his turtle house. I then headed out the door, back towards my place. I walked a little ways, then stopped to listen for the bear. I didn't hear anything, so I ambled on, walking on the fresh snow—I love to walk atop a new snowfall—like to hear it crunch under my feet. I always grab up a handful and taste it too—still a lot of little boy in me, I guess.

"Anyway, I was about half way home when I started to hear that old, familiar growling once again. That bear was closer than before, and sounded a lot unfriendlier! I stopped dead in my tracks, trying to figure out just exactly where he was. Sound doesn't have much direction in the fog. It's hard to tell where a noise is actually coming from. Snow kept getting into my eyes too. I was—wait a minute—somebody on the road up front of us there..."

The young trio's eyes quickly turned onto the road ahead, where a man on a painted horse approached them. The man was dressed in deerskin, and there were three eagle feathers on one side of his head, protrudin' upward from a rounded piece of leather that was somehow attached to his hair.

He soon raised his right hand in their direction, palm open, his fingers pointin' upward—an Indian's greetin', my Dad told me, meanin' that he was a man of peaceful intentions. He said nothin', nary a word, as he rode slowly toward the wagon, his hand still in the air for a bit. My Dad watched with great interest—though a mite skittish at the time, he was really gettin' in to his western experience.

Jeremiah spoke suddenly and a bit loudly at the rider, startlin' the trio, while at the same time raisin' a hand in like manner toward the man.

"Na-shees-ta-shay! Hello my friend! —Don't worry, kids —it's John Windwalker, a good friend of mine. Don't be scared of the way he looks. He's a Crow Indian and really a gentle fellow, when you get to know him. He's the best man *I* know, though his father and I were once upon a time mortal enemies—tooth and nail type stuff!. He knew you were coming, and I'm sure he's here to greet you."

Hannah clung to Carrie, somewhat fearful of this stranger, who was fierce lookin' indeed. His face was ruddy and sharp featured underneath a shimmering flow of black hair that fell well below his shoulders. Most strikin' was a long, coarse scar on the left side of his cheek that ran downward and onto his neck. There were more facial scars, his eyes were narrow and a mite piercin', and the man didn't smile. But the eagle feathers arrayed as they were in his hair were notably handsome.

Still not speakin', he eyed the girls for a brief time as his mount drew near. He was approachin' on the left side of the wagon, and then rode around behind it and on up the right side, reinin' into a slowed pace right beside my Dad. His painted mount then kept in step with the team of horses. Them animals seemed untroubled by his approach and present movement. The Indian eyed the girls once again, and then looked directly at my Dad.

Aunt Carrie finally managed to say, "Hello, sir."

The Indian then addressed Jeremiah. "That's the first time anyone ever called me 'sir' since I knowed ya," he smiled.

When his smile broke, both Carrie and Hannah relaxed. My Dad was still a bit nervous, this fierce lookin' fella' ridin' right next to him and all. He scooted across the bench, a bit closer to Jeremiah.

"Are you a real Indian?"

John Windwalker laughed as he stroked the hair from his eyes and leaned in toward the wagon, both hands then on the horn of his saddle. He looked right into Carrie's eyes, who had asked that question. There had been no echo from Hannah this time—too much in awe over the personal appearance of the man. My Dad had remained silent as well.

"I think so," he replied. "I'm not a good one, though, because I am not dead yet."

His remark seemed to go over the youngster's heads. There were a lot of folks around the country in the older days who figured the only good Indian was a dead one. But, with the Indian wars at an end, new folks movin' west come to find the Indian culture mighty interestin'. I figure they could have seen that a long time ago—might have avoided all them crazy wars, had they just accepted the Indians and not tried to make 'em white.

"Johnson," he said. "There's a couple men up at your cabin —white men. I do not know who they are—I have never seen them around here. They were looking into the windows when I rode up. They backed off right away when they saw me. Asked me if I knowed Jeremiah Johnson.

"I says, 'who don't?' I told them you were probably on your way back from Independence. I told them I was riding out to meet you. Told them you had your nieces and nephew with you. They did not seem too happy, and they acted like they'd never seen an Indian before—either that, or they had seen one and don't particularly like them.

"I don't think they liked me much. I told them they could ride along with me, if they was a' mind to. They said they'd just wait there—I backed my horse up a' ways. Didn't feel like turning my back on them. I looked around and did not see anything out of place on your ranch. Then I rode out, headed your way."

"What did they look like?" Johnson asked.

"One of them was lean, but had a big belly. The other was a bigger fellow—wide-shouldered and a bit taller. Both looked like they'd been in the saddle awhile. The taller man had a tattoo on the top of his left hand. Looked like a cross or something similar. I could not see it clearly from the back of my mount. This man wore a strange hat."

"Who do you think they are, Uncle Jeremiah?" Carrie asked.

Johnson hesitated. "It's hard telling. Perhaps some folks I knew a while back. Maybe when I lived in the Rockies."

"Was that after you left Ohio, Uncle Jeremiah?"

"Yes—many years after I left Ohio." Johnson was deep in thought. The others could tell by the expression on his face, and asked no more questions at that particular moment.

"Let's get going. We'll be at the cabin shortly," he said.

"I'll ride along with you," the Indian encouraged.

"Will you finish the story about the bear, Uncle Jeremiah?" Young Hannah spoke up with much eagerness in her voice.

Jeremiah turned his head toward the girls. They were smilin', both hopin' that he would continue to enlighten them. He glanced over at my young Dad, who still had his eyes on Windwalker, now captivated by his presence, and more at ease with his rugged manner and the direct way in which he spoke about things.

He'd never seen no one like him before, bein' from Ohio and all—none of those children had. There wasn't no Indians left in the Ohio country in them days—none anyway that rode a painted horse, dressed head to toe in deerskin, wore eagle's feathers in their hair, and had scars all over their face like this John Windwalker did.

Trailside Meadow, just above the Johnson Ranch

The Two Strangers
Chapter 2

Jeremiah shook the reins gently and the horse team increased their pace. His thoughts were on those men waitin' at the ranch, but he didn't let on none.

"Sure, I can finish the story for you. —Like I said, I stood there in the fog, unsure of just where that bear was. His growling put him within fifty or sixty feet of me. It seemed like it was more behind me than in front of me, but like I said before, it's hard to tell about sound in the fog. I decided to just keep walking on ahead. I knew the cabin wasn't much further.

"I then got the notion to start making some noise! Usually, if you make a lot of noise, a bear will run off. So, that's what I did. I started woopin' and hollerin' as loud as I could, while moving a mite quicker toward the cabin—broke into an all out run, actually. All of a sudden there was the cabin door. I jerked it open in a hurry, stepped inside and closed it just as quick. I no sooner got that oak bar in place when, wham! That bear must have hit that door with all four's.

"There was no way he was going to get through it. I heard him sniff around for a bit, pawin' at the door and growlin' a mite, then he wandered off, thank God. I remembered just at that time about a bear coming through a cabin door when I was up in Colorado, no thanks to an old hunter named Chris Lapp. Bear Claw was the fellow's nickname—but that's another story —we'll save that one for fireside."

"You were lucky, Uncle Jeremiah!" Carrie spoke up, shakin' her head in wonder.

Hannah was clingin' tightly to her sister's coat, and echoed, "You were lucky, Uncle Jeremiah." She then asked him, "Did the bear ever come back?"

"He was gone by first light, Hannah. Snow had covered his tracks and I wasn't sure where he wandered off to. Several bears are still around, but we're not sure if that particular bear is one of them. Nobody's been attacked—the bears have kept their distance. None of them are real big, but the one that hit my door that night was a huge fellow. There were some cookies in my coat pocket—found them later and forgot I'd put 'em in there. I figure that's what he was after.

"I'm not sure where he went, and it's a mite hard to find a grizz when you're out there looking for one—it's when you're *not* looking for them that they find you. It's been about a year ago, now. I figure he's still around somewhere, though. Hopefully he's found a good home. They like this Sierra country, and I can't blame them one bit. It's a mighty hearty country, and there's plenty of food for those critters."

Two men could be seen sittin' on the front porch when Johnson's wagon and Windwalker's mount reached the crest of a rise, where the cabin and a good part of the ranch come into view on the ridge below. Jeremiah brought the wagon to a halt atop the crest. He squinted his eyes while in thought, lookin' down at those men for a bit, and then spoke at Windwalker.

"I know those men, John. We're a ways off, but I think the one on the left—the bigger fellow—is ol' Railroad Ron. That strange hat you mentioned is sure enough a railroader's cap. He was with the Union Pacific when I left Colorado. The other fellow looks like Ed Shay, a lawman from down southern California way—a good one. Comes up here on occasion to fish the high lakes."

Johnson paused for a moment, lookin' back down at those men. Then he said, "Can't figure out how those two got together, or why they would be up here—especially this time of year?"

30

"Your eyes see much, Johnson—like the eagle. I cannot see clearly such a great distance. You figure it's trouble?" the Indian questioned. "I can scare them off from here—and real easy." He put a hand on the butt of a Winchester rifle that was tied to his saddle rig.

"I don't think so," Johnson laughed. "I saved ol' Ron's life one time. Some Indian chief had captured him and tied him to a tree in Rattlesnake Canyon—chief name of Mad Wolf. He'd been bitten three times when I found him. He was one sorry looking individual. I sucked out the poison, best I could, then put him across my saddle and rode into Flathead country, just above Wolf Tail Valley—you know the place, John.

"Two Tongues Labeau was chief of the Flathead at the time, and nursed him back to health. He rode with me for about a month after that, then got up one morning and said he was headed for Denver. I rode with him to the rail-head in Durango —never saw him after that. As for Shay, he was fishing up here in the high country when I met him for the first time. That was three summers ago."

Windwalker relaxed in the saddle. "Well, I guess we'll ride on in there and find out just what they want."

"I guess we will," Johnson nodded, starting the team up again.

"Railroad Ron?" Carrie questioned. "Does he have another name, or a last name?"

Jeremiah glanced back at her as he shook the reins. "I don't know—never asked him."

A short time later, Railroad Ron and Ed Shay stepped off the porch and approached the wagon just as Johnson and the trio pulled up. Windwalker dismounted there and helped Carrie and Hannah down from the wagon.

31

"Good to see you, Jeremiah," Ron said, extending a hand toward him. Johnson shook his hand, then in turn shook the hand of Ed Shay.

"Good to see both of you boys. What brings you up here? You two know each other?"

Railroad Ron spoke first on that matter. I never knew Railroad Ron or Ed Shay, personally, but Dad spoke of them often after he told me this story, and spoke well of them. They're no longer alive, not in the flesh anyway—it's been a long time ago now, but this story keeps them alive for me. They were special men—God fearin' men. That's dang rare now a' days. Some men boast they're God fearin', but sure don't live it.

"I retired from the railroad about a year or so ago. You know how things were in Colorado, Jeremiah—with all the people pourin' in, killin' off game, puttin' up towns and such. Just had my fill, I guess. Went into Nevada for a spell and took up prospecting. After all those difficult years with the railroad, it was good just to wander and relax—to enjoy this here creation of God's, and just live off the land one day at a time.

"Then I heard there was a lot of gold here in the Sierras, so I bought me a good horse in Battle Mountain and rode west. Talked to a trapper in Reno, who said he heard that you were in or near Lone Pine—somewhere a'bout's. So, I headed this way. I figgered if anyone could lead me to gold, you could! Met up with Shay here at June Lake. Took to him right away," he smiled.

"He's a likable fellow. You're not a lawman anymore?" Johnson inquired toward Shay.

"Retired three months ago," Ed replied. "You know me— don't like to stay in one place for very long, now that I'm older. The saddle suits me just fine. A day after I retired I just headed north from the Basin to my old camp at June. I met this railroadin', sodbustin' tracklayer, and gold sounded like a good

32

thing." He smiled at Ron momentarily, with a jestin' left handed punch against his shoulder, and then continued his words with Johnson.

"We figured we'd come down here and see if we could talk you into guiding us over the Sierras into Mineral King. We heard there was gold there, and dang few prospectors. Sounded like the kind of odds we were looking for, considering that we're looking more for relaxation than we are for gold. Lord knows we don't need money. Just some peace and freedom—and adventure, of course," he laughed.

"We know how well you know these mountains, Johnson. Knowing your spirit, we figured you might even like to tag along. Figured you might like to get away from the madness for a while—people pourin' in and bringin' in their eastern ways. Lord knows you're the best guide there is in these parts —in a lot of parts for that matter, though I did hear that John Muir was wandering these mountains somewhere here a'bout's. Shared a campfire with a couple ol' boys up Yosemite way—they said he was somewhere up there in the rocks."

Johnson grinned. "John Muir? I guided him up Mt. Whitney a few years back. That fellow became right popular after that. Did a lot of writing and encouraging folks back east about the High Sierras. Had a little population explosion after that too. I wasn't happy about it at the time, but a lot of nice folks have settled in the area. Most of them respect the high country.

"Buried a few of them a while back—after an earthquake hit. Folks around here were okay, but some of the Lone Pine residents didn't make it. I didn't know any of them—migrant workers mostly. Some of the markers over there don't have any names on them. Sad thing, it was. But that's how life is sometimes in this country. It's a fine country, but a hard life for

33

some folks more than others—nature's got its own way with each of 'em."

"How about Clarence King?" Ron asked. "We heard he had a tough time findin' the correct route to Whitney—least ways that's what the newspapers said, back in Denver and places."

"That he did!" Johnson laughed. "I think he made at least four attempts before he finally chose the right pass and found his way to the summit. A local group of fishermen got the credit for the very first climb, about a month before King made it, though he was one of the first white men to climb in this area as well.

"Of course, most of them don't know I was up there long before any of them, and I know of a couple Indians who made the climb before any white men ever set foot into this area. The Spanish were here a hundred or so years before that. I think they hiked the White Mountains, to the east over there—some Spanish relics have been found—don't know if they wandered the Sierras at all—no sign of them ever being here. I guess it doesn't matter anyway. The good Lord saw it all before any of them, or us—He formed it."

"And some fine sculpturing He did," Shay added.

The talkin' stopped momentarily as the group looked about at the surroundin' mountains. Carrie, Marc and Hannah had been listenin' intently to the conversation between the men. They now shared with them their immediate attention to the breathtakin' scenery that overlooked the big valley of the Johnson ranch.

Ain't no better escarpment of white granite in the entire world like the Eastern Sierra. John Windwalker too joined in their pause to gaze upon the majesty of those granite wonders. My dad watched him—said Windwalker held his head high and breathed in the air, like the mountains was a part of him and was what kept him alive. After a few moments he broke, with respect, into everyone's silence.

"I know of this Muir. He is a friend of the local Indian people. He has said that it seemed to him that the Sierra should not be called the Nevada or the Snowy Range, but the Range of Light. And, after ten years spent in the heart of it—seeing the sunbursts of morning among the icy peaks, the noonday radiance on the trees and rocks and snow, the flush of the alpenglow—it still seemed to him above all others the Range of Light; the most divinely beautiful of all the mountain chains he has ever seen. The man is well acquainted with the Great Spirit —he could see Him in the rocks as he journeyed through here and walked among them."

"He is indeed wise," Johnson breathed, "the kind of a man that might lead the charge against those high-binders in Washington, who want to ravage these forests and move the rocks all around. He's a man who believes in keeping this land the way we found it. Be a sin for anyone to civilize these mountains. They say he's friends with the President. Maybe he can put a stop to the madness before it happens."

All continued to stand and gaze in silence for still several moments longer, each of them appreciatin' things in their own way. Carrie was inspired to move close and put one arm around her uncle, while holdin' onto Hannah's hand. Her presence at that moment prompted him to introduce the children to Railroad Ron and Ed Shay.

"These are my kin—my only nephew and two nieces. They've come all the way from Ohio to spend some time with me. A long, overdue visit. I don't think I will have the time to guide you boys up there just now, though I do have that inclination. Those mountains have a way of beckoning one to climb on up and taste their grandeur. They speak to me every day that I'm in this part of the country."

Jeremiah was itchin' to go, that's for sure, but he had to be firm with himself and quickly moved his train of thought to considerin' the presence of his kin—his only blood family.

"No—can't do it just now, boys. I've got these fine looking youngsters to watch after right now. It's a dream come true, actually."

Railroad Ron spoke up. "They're mighty pretty girls—and that's a smart lookin' boy there too. He don't say much, but his eyes been fixed on them mountains ever since he got here, and that says a lot. I'm sure your time together with these young'uns will be precious. What chance do we have of findin' our own way, Jeremiah?"

"Little—or none," Johnson replied.

"How long does it take to get up and over to Mineral King?"

"Two days up to the John Muir Trail, then it's an easy ride down into the canyon of Mineral King. Problem is, the trails are not marked all too well. You could get lost pretty easy up there. Those sharp peaks, the *Needles* they call them, show no mercy. It's easy to get disoriented among the outcrops that surround them and end up goin' in circles. Snow can get a mite deep up that high too. But I understand you wanting to find gold. Had me a little strike over there myself, several years back—that's how I got this ranch."

"Let's go with them, uncle Jeremiah," Carrie suddenly urged.

Them words sure caught him by surprise. "We came out here to hike with you," she continued. Rain and snow doesn't matter to us. It snows all the time back in Ohio—there's tornadoes and big rain storms as well—thunder and lightning and all that stuff."

Johnson looked at her, then at Hannah. He glanced down at my Dad, who stood close to him. Hopeful anticipation was written all over their faces. Johnson knew that at Hannah's age she would agree with 'bout anything Carrie suggested, and my Dad, well, he was a spirited young lad, yet was somewhat quiet in his demeanor, a trait that ol' Railroad Ron and Jeremiah had both picked up on and considered a great strength. There was nothin' wrong with quiet.

Ol' Jeremiah just smiled and shook his head. "Well, the Lord does work in mysterious ways. —It will be cold," he warned. "And it won't be easy—no church social. You gals are a bit young, especially Hannah here. Marc is young as well. But, I guess the experience you kids might gain would last a lifetime.

"Experience is what life's all about, I reckon. I know the neighbor boys have been wanting to go up over the mountain. Might be more fun for you youngsters if they were to tag along. You all might tend to think less about the cold or any hardship we may run into."

Johnson turned his head 'n eyes toward the high peaks, contemplatin' for a few moments—wonderin' if his offer was such a good idea. His partiality to his niece's wishes, along with the pull of his own heart, could turn out to be costly.

The high trails were no bowl of cherries, that's for sure—and winter was a' comin' on. The high country can get mighty rough in winter—unrelentin' at times. A body could freeze or get injured or killed by wild animals. But, bein' that Jeremiah would be with 'em, their chances at survival would at least go from none to better.

"We would appreciate it, Johnson," Ed Shay encouraged. "These kids would be fine company—might give me a chance to use my grandpa skills," he laughed. "I think it would be one fine trek, providing we don't get scalped, killed or freeze to death—no offense, Indian." He smiled slightly at Windwalker, feeling a little skittish about what he had just said.

Johnson laughed. "Sorry. I'm not much with introductions. This is John Windwalker. He's of the Crow Nation. He came here with me from Colorado. And don't worry, there's no wild Indians in the Sierras—least not lately. Just a few explorers and trappers here and there.

"Most of them are friendly. Now and then you'll run across some thieves and robbers—there's always sinners here a'bout's. Biggest threat up there is of course the bears. They don't take too kindly to trespassing into their domain. Might run into a wolf or two as well, maybe even a mountain lion. I've met them all before—I'm still here."

He ran his hand through Hannah's hair and winked at Carrie. "The trail's a bit craggy, though, which makes the goin' rough. And we're due a good snow. Let's go on into the cabin. We can cook up some dinner and talk this thing over. We should make some plans and consider the proper gear we'll need to take along on this journey."

He then nodded once at the group, a gesture of his confidence in what he had just proposed. "Wind's picking up. Come along inside. Clouds are forming over the northern peaks —might get some rain directly down here in the valley. Storms can come over those mountains before you know it."

An old mountain man once said, 'You can't predict a mountain nor cheat it. The mountain's got their own way.' Jeremiah knew this well. For him there was much to consider. The horses, mules and supplies were no problem, but the weather could be. The safety of his own kin and that of his friends was at the front of his thinkin'.

Rain wouldn't be so bad, but lightnin' strikes were common along the higher elevations, 'specially near the Needles. Snow would be an even greater danger, impairin' their journey and possibly any immediate retreat that they might be forced to make.

The group discussed each of these things over a fine steak and beans dinner. The hot cornbread also was a real treat for my Dad and the girls, and there was plenty of it. Nothin' like a good mountain man's dinner in them days to nourish and strengthen a body, and Jeremiah had become quite a good cook over the years. He always said that 'a man can't work well on poor feed.' Besides, he was the kind of man who would take good care of his own kin, and this visit from his brother's kids was for sure one of the better times in his life. Letters to my Dad from him told me that in no uncertain terms.

Jeremiah later took the trio down the road to meet the Perez family, and to inquire about Bryce and Cael Perez taggin' along on the journey. But, the Perez family was expectin' company. Their cousins, Riley Virginia, Mikey, and Joseph, were about to descend on 'em. Mr. Perez and his wife, Sheri, also added that keepin' a needed eye 'bout Bryce and Cael on that high trail was too heavy a burden for Jeremiah—could be more than a passel full of trouble.

Of course in those days and in that high country, you could trust no man better than Jeremiah Johnson, and the Perez family knew that quite well. But, the High Sierra trail was not an easy trek—not one bit. A few full grow'd men had disappeared along that trail. Bears, wolves and mountain lions were seen crossin' it many a'time in search of food, and all sorts of accidents among men were common as well.

Outlaws were known to ride the high trail now and then. Some folks had even been robbed at gunpoint up there. Then there was the legend of an ol' crazy man, who roamed the mountains and was said to have killed folks for the gold in their teeth. They said he cut off their heads and picked the gold teeth out of their mouths with a knife. A ghastly fellow for sure, legend be true.

It was just at sunset when Jeremiah and the kids left the Perez place and headed on back to the ranch. Ed Shay and Railroad Ron were sittin' on the porch havin' a smoke when they come back. Windwalker was just ridin' through the gate about the same time, havin' just returned from watchin' the sunset on Coyote Mesa. He liked to listen to the wind up there too. He also talked to the trees and the rocks and claimed that they spoke back at him. As time went on he taught my Dad a lot about things like that.

Windwalker rode on up to the porch where everyone was gathered, and spoke from atop his mount. "Looks like there is much snow in the rocks that embrace the Needles," he said, lookin' up at 'em over his shoulder. "Full moon is rising, though—and I saw a hawk on the wind—both of these are a good sign."

John Windwalker knew about signs. You've got to be an Indian to know those things. Indian's are not like whites—they know where the center of the earth is, and they live by that wisdom. They honor all things created by the Great Spirit[1], and commune with nature. Their celebrations, customs and practices keep their lives focused on a higher power—the one true God who made everything on the earth and in the heavens. They keep alert to the presence of the dark forces as well, whom they know exist. They are a rare breed of folks.

There's a lot of philosophies and religions in our world today—people thinkin' and practicin' all kinds of things. But I swear, ain't none of 'em understands the earth, its elements—wind, rain and such, and all the other things that God made—none of 'em understands these wonders and how to draw knowledge from 'em like the Native Americans. It's that particular quality that makes 'em a mighty honorable people. Someday these least among the nations may be pronounced the greatest in the heavens.

Jeremiah built a bonfire just after sunset, in celebration of the youngsters bein' at the ranch for the very first time. They was up for quite some time that night and kept the fire burnin'. They talked about lots of things and everyone, young and old alike, had a part in the conversations.

John Windwalker wanted to cap off the night with a dance around the fire—somethin' he said his people did in the old days, whenever there was somethin' meaningful to celebrate.

He said he was saddened that the great fires of celebration could no longer be seen across the land.

Well, he taught everyone there somethin' that night. He had all the men a' howlin' at the moon, had them youngsters chantin' at the stars, and taught everybody the meanin' behind it all. He said it was heartfelt praise to the Great Spirit who made all things.

He said it honored God for allowin' the children to journey safely across the country and be a part of the great West. He said that they were special children—destined for this particular time and place, and that even greater things awaited them.

He was quite right, considerin' the way things turned out. Like I said, you gotta' be an Indian to know those things.

The town of Big Pine, in the old days, lookin' east from the cemetery toward the White Mountains

Robbery at Big Pine
Chapter 3

The next mornin' Ed Shay could smell the dyin' embers of that memorable fire as he stepped into the corral and saddled his horse. It was a fine, exhilaratin' scent, and it would prove to be a fine and invigoratin' day as well—not a cloud in the sky. The early mornin' sun was not yet above the horizon, but its increasin' light cast shades of purple on the white granite of the Sierras, which caught the attention of the man. He looked over top the saddle at the light display as he tightened a harness strap.

The awe of the early mornin' spectacle caused him to pause leisurely as he stood next to his mount, at that time restin' both his hands atop the saddle. He was for a few brief moments caught in the beauty of the mornin', and I for one can't blame him. Mornin's anywhere are indeed a grand thing, but in the Sierras, the scent of a previous night's campfire embracin' a clear mornin' and its sunrise is downright exquisite.

The Sierra Nevada are solid granite, a vast deposit of huge, white blocks and boulders that stretch for hundreds of miles through California, dividin' its richly soiled farmlands on the west from its rugged deserts to the east. Above the timberline its seemin'ly infinite, lofty crags and pointed, white buttes tower over 14,000 feet into the sky, and can literally take one's breath away in no time at all.

The purple skies of the early mornin' add a serenity to the place that, as I've been told, is unequaled anywhere in the country. Ed Shay was captivated by this serenity for a time—he later said it was like time had actually stopped long enough for him to get a fix on his soul that he never had before. He said it was the first time he'd ever thought he knew for sure that there was a God. While thinkin' intently on these things he heard the corral gate openin' behind him.

"I swear." The voice was that of Railroad Ron. "Nothin' like a sunrise on the High Sierra. I spent years in Colorado, Ed, and the Rockies are fine specimens indeed, with their steep slopes and unendin' forests and all, but the granite boulders that make up the Sierra Nevada are down right captivatin', 'specially this time of day. That Muir fellow was darn right—a range of light it is!"

"That he was," Ed replied.

Railroad Ron walked on into the corral and stood beside him. "Goin' for an early ride, are ya?"

"Yes Sir. I thought I might ride off to town and pick up some more personal supplies for the journey. Johnson still wants to leave tomorrow, don't he?"

"That's what he said. I'm ready right now," Ron laughed.

Ed Shay nodded his head in agreement. "Me too—you need anything from town?"

"Not really, but I'll ride in with ya. That hardware store in Big Pine is sure to have somethin' I'll want. Whether I'll really need it or not is another story."

"I hear you—what's Johnson doing?"

"Him and the young ones are cookin' up some pancakes and bacon. I sure wouldn't mind gettin' a bite or two before we ride off to town," Ron said, rubbing the whiskers on his chin. He had a habit of doin' that chin rubbin' routine whenever he suggested an idea that he wanted anyone to agree to. If they didn't agree, he would usually go his own way anyway. He wasn't a man to push any sort of idea on another, but he was a bit set in his ways about most things. He figured he had earned that right over the years. The man had a lot of experience in life. 'Lot of sand,' is what I'd call it.

He was somewhat gruff and was known to swear on occasion, but Jeremiah Johnson was one man who had learned to value his opinion. Ed Shay didn't really know him all that well just yet. But he would get to know him, over time, and that friendship would last until the very end of their lives.

"Sounds good," Ed agreed. "We'll saddle your horse and then go in and get some of that breakfast. A man that don't eat pancakes of a mornin' is missing a good thing—besides, I can smell that bacon now—in no way can I ride away from that without a taste of it."

"You think Johnson can cook?" Ron laughed, knowin' in reality the he had eaten quite well with him back on the Colorado trails.

Shay snickered a bit. "I don't suppose there's anything he can't do, but I'm sure you know that. I'm glad he's going with us. We were lucky to find him at home, you know that?"

Ron nodded. "I'm glad too. Hell, somebody might ask me someday, 'Did you really ride over the Sierras with Jeremiah Johnson?' And I can say, 'Yep—I rode all over the high and mighty Sierras with Jeremiah Johnson.'"

Ed shook his head in agreement. "A-men, brother. A-men."

Inside the cabin Johnson and the youngsters had finished cookin' the bacon and had a fine stack of pancakes on a plate and another stack in the makin'. The aroma that had enticed those cowboys was much stronger when the two men opened the front door of the cabin and crossed the floor into the kitchen.

"You boys hungry?" Johnson grinned.

"You could say that," Ron answered. "The smell of those pancakes and bacon remind me of a little greasy spoon in Reno. I hit that town early one mornin' and followed that scent near a mile 'till I found the place. That ol' gal that was doin' the cookin' wasn't too happy with me, though.

"After I ate my fill I says to her, 'Thank you ma'am, that was right tasty.' She got an old scowl on her face and she says, 'I was beginnin' to think you didn't like it—you only 'et four plates!' So I says to her, 'Well, it ain't good to eat too much on an empty stomach, ma'am.' She looked a bit disgusted—I got to thinkin' about it, after that remark, and did pay her a little extra money for her time and trouble."

"No charge here," Johnson laughed. "You eat that much, you can wash dishes instead."

"No problem. Ed and me are figgerin' on ridin' off to town after breakfast—after them dishes are done, of course. Anything you need, Jeremiah?"

"Can I go?" my aunt Carrie interrupted excitedly.

"Why sure, girl," Ron answered. "It's all right, ain't it Jeremiah?"

"Fine," he answered. "I'm going to take Marc and Hannah back over to the Perez place today. Sheri Perez is packing us some goodies for the journey. I'll have John Windwalker saddle a horse for Carrie."

He looked over at John, who was squatted down by the fireplace, quietly enjoying his breakfast. "The grey will do for her, John—he's gentle enough."

"I'll go outside with him," Carrie added. "I can saddle a horse quite well, Uncle Jeremiah—if he can just show me where all the gear is hanging?"

"He can do that," Johnson nodded.

When Ron, Ed, and Carrie finally did hit the road to Big Pine the sun had made its way a short distance above the horizon. It was incredibly warm for a December mornin'. The smell of juniper and sage along the ol' road was indeed an inspiration to the senses.

As they left the ridge of the Johnson ranch, Carrie's gray mount strode between those of the two men. Once they began the long, downward slope toward Big Pine itself, the horses, encouraged by their riders, were none-to-soon off to a gallop. Some joyous laughter arose among the group as they endeavored to turn the ride to town into a race, along with a back and forth challenge of stunts and a few show-off routines. Ol' Railroad Ron was famous for stunt-ridin'—grew up in a stable, I was told. Busted broncs' and trained horses for some well-to-do folks when he was just a young man—that was before the Indian wars.

Carrie rode well for her age and the two men were none to shy to praise her about it. When the horses began to tire and the pace ramped down again, some deeper conversation ensued among the three, who had slowed the animals to a walk and were ridin' abreast just a mile or two from the town of Big Pine. That last portion of the road was a long, flat stretch, straight 'n wide, and you could see the town's buildin's in the distance. Railroad Ron started the conversation.

"How long has it been since you seen your uncle?" he asked, directin' the question at my aunt Carrie.

"This is the first time ever," she answered. "Uncle Jeremiah left Ohio and went off to war long before I was born. He was just a boy—sixteen, I think. He went into the Rockies after he mustered out. He had an Indian wife and sort of adopted a white son he had found at a massacre in Colorado. That's what my dad told me.

"Not long after the three of them settled in up there, he led some soldiers through a sacred burial ground, to save some settlers who were stranded in the mountains. The Indians didn't like what he did, so they raided Uncle Jeremiah's cabin and killed his Indian wife and the boy. We never knew his wife's name. Caleb was the boy's name. Uncle Jeremiah had named him—I don't really know anymore about him or her.

"Anyway, I was told he spent years fighting those Indians after that happened. He got out of the mountains eventually and went down to a town. My dad said he didn't like it there, so he drifted up to Canada. He was a wanderer! My dad never heard from him again 'till after I was born. He started writing to my dad more often after that. My dad said that Uncle Jeremiah seemed different somehow—more affable.

"He told dad in a letter that he was leaving Canada and going out to California. We were living in Ohio by that time—that's where Uncle Jeremiah and my dad grew up. I was just two years old when we moved there from Boston, and dad wanted to bring me out lots of times, but we just never came. Then Marc was born, then later, Hannah. We never seemed to have the time to make the trip during those years. My mom never wanted to come anyway—said it was too wild in the West.

"But, this year was different! Dad had saved enough for our trip, my mom gave in, and here I am—here we are! My dad has a real good business in Ohio—sells farming equipment. He gave Marc, Hannah and me some extra money, bought us some new clothes, and then put us on a train. I know one thing—I sure am glad we could come—I never saw such beautiful country as this California!"

My aunt Carrie's words were mixed with emotions of both sadness and joy. She wiped her eyes and smiled at the men, then quickly gained her composure in a brief silence that followed. She was soon at ease again.

"Have you known my Uncle Jeremiah long?" she presently inquired of Railroad Ron. "And, by the way, if you don't mind me asking, do you have a last name?"

"Nope—don't mind—but there's no last name. My folks were kilt when I was just a young'un. Some horse breeders took me in, but never give me no name. They just called me 'Ron.' Their last name was 'Friend.' I guess they didn't know if I'd grow up to be friend or foe," he laughed, "so they never give me their name. I was a mite ornery—I really don't think they liked me much anyhow—nope—never did.

"Some good ol' boys give me the name 'Railroad Ron' when I went to work for the Union Pacific. They had two or three 'Ron's' workin' for 'em in that outfit at the time, and figgered if I wanted to get paid, I'd best have a proper name. I been goin' by 'Railroad Ron' ever since. Ain't no mistaken after that about who I am. I like the name—it fits alright.

"As for your uncle, I knew him in Colorado. He saved my life when a band of wild Indians near kilt me. They left me for the rattlesnakes, but ol' Jeremiah come on my predicament and made stew outa' them critters. I rode with him for a spell after that. It was the Crow Indians that were bent on doin' him in—come after him one at a time—for a couple years. That was all right, he was lucky—Apaches would have sent fifty at once. A chief name of Paints-His-Shirt-Red was the culprit. Did your dad tell you anything about him?"

"No. Dad doesn't talk much about those years. I'm not sure what he knows either—I've never read any of the letters Uncle Jeremiah sent to him. I would have liked to, but dad said I was too young to read some of the things he wrote about."

"Well, like I said, Paints-His-Shirt sent his braves after Jeremiah for desecratin' that burial ground you mentioned. Try as they might they couldn't defeat him. Finally, the chief himself went out to hunt Jeremiah. Found him in the high country above the Wolf Tail Valley. They fought with one another tooth and nail, and Jeremiah won out in the end, standin' over top of Paints-His-Shirt with a knife.

"Said he wanted to stick him real good and turn the knife every which a' way—wanted to cut his heart out, but told me that somethin' inside himself said that enough was enough—he was 'tired of hating', he told me. He said he just dropped the knife on the ground and rode off. Paints-His-Shirt never bothered him again after that. I figger his life bein' spared by a great warrior like your uncle was a powerful sign to Paints-His-Shirt. Injun's are real spiritual folk. In fact, he swore to protect Jeremiah from that day on."

Ed Shay was as much into Ron's words as was my aunt Carrie. "How's that?" he asked.

"Windwalker," Ron answered. "That's Paints-His-Shirt's son. I never saw him face to face until now, but heard tell of him. His Indian name is Walks-With-The-Wind. When Paints-His-Shirt died some years later, he made his son swear to protect Johnson. He made him swear to never leave Johnson's side until he saved his life—at least once. That was his dyin' request—his last words to his own son! Quite a turnaround in attitude for an Injun—but they got their own ways."

"Really?" Carrie breathed. "So Windwalker came west with Uncle Jeremiah then—from Colorado?"

"Looks that way. I don't know about that part—don't know if they were in Canada together, just heard about the vow from an old trapper." Railroad Ron weaved the leather reins of his horse back and forth through his broad fingers as he talked and rode. "A fella name of Del Gue—a French fella. I guess he rode with Jeremiah for a spell in the early days—before Jeremiah met the Indian lady.

"He was a wild one, that Del Gue. But he said that Jeremiah taught him to care about the mountain critters. Ol' Del said he learned to talk to 'em after that. Said he'd been talkin' to himself for years, and so was glad to have the company. But, like I said, he was a wild one—and loved to pull a cork."

The trio became silent as they entered the outskirts of Big Pine, ridin' in step together with the warm sun against their backs. There were several people comin' into town on that early mornin'—an unusual thing for midweek. But, there were a lot more folks comin' west in those days. The railroads made that possible, and the High Sierras was the destination for folks who wanted to settle in where they could view the white granite.

50

There were even more people within the town itself when Ron, Ed, and Carrie rode in on Main Street. They were takin' in everything along the way—lookin' at all the names on the buildin's and such, and could see a large group gathered in front of the bank, way down at the end of the street, as they neared the center of town. Ed Shay was the first to speak.

"Looks like there may have been a robbery. I'm going to ride on up there—be back in a minute or two."

"Don't be ridin' off—we got to get supplies," Ron warned.

Ed looked back at him as he rode off. "Well, what's keepin' ya?"

Once a lawman, always a lawman. Ed Shay had it in his blood. We all reach for somethin' to hold onto in life—especially when we get older. Somethin' with meanin' that may continue to sustain us, when we actually no longer have it. Ed had that for sure.

He was a fine lawman in his day, no doubt about that. And bein' a lawman was indeed an honor to look back on. It takes a special breed. You've got to be tough at times, yet tender at other times. You need the ability to deal honestly, fairly and justly, while in a position of power—that's a hard find in a man. Ed still loved the excitement of it all as well.

He spurred his horse and trotted on over to the crowd in quick fashion. As he approached the nearby buildin's, he saw a heavyset man with a black mustache come out of the bank. Some people were talkin' to him, pushin' up real close to him. Ed recognized him right off. The man saw Ed out of the corner of his eye and turned from the crowd to speak to him.

"Ed Shay! I swear!"

The man was Ken Petty, sheriff of Big Pine. A tough old boy, who had worked in Los Angeles with Ed several years back. He got tired of that wild town, moved north, and was eventually elected sheriff in Big Pine. When he wasn't sheriffin', he was out fishin' the local creeks. He was in the

51

right part of the country for it, that's for sure. But, he was known to mix business with pleasure now and again. There was a time or two that he would sneak off and fish while on duty.

Ed later told Railroad Ron and Carrie that Sheriff Petty was out fishin' on such an occasion, when a bunch of drunk cowboys started shootin' at one another out in back of the Big Pine Saloon. When the town mayor finally found the sheriff at Rush Creek, ol' Petty took one hand off the fishin' pole and begun waivin' the mayor away, tellin' him to ride on back to town—said, 'Let them boys have their fun. We'll gather up the bodies and read over 'em in the mornin'—I got me a *big* fish nibblin' at this line today—ain't no call for me to be a' ridin' off to town to bandy words with drunkards!'

As it turned out, nobody got hurt. None of them shooters could hit what they were aimin' at in the first place. When they did fire off the few cartridges that was in their guns they was too drunk to reload. So, them boys just sat around jawin' for a spell and eventually passed out. Some pranksters shoveled horse dung all over 'em in the middle of the night—covered 'em from head to toe.

Some folks think ol' Petty had somethin' to do with that. Ed figures they were right—the ol' boy loved to play jokes on cowboys. Sheriff Petty said when he found 'em the next mornin', the flies were so thick that the fire department had to come and hose the men down. But ol' Petty just sprouted a wide grin and said that the big fish that he'd finally reeled in was worth more than any of the trouble that followed.

"Howdy, Ken," Ed nodded. "What's goin' on here?"
"There's been a robbery, Ed. You still wearin' a badge?"
"No sir, retired a few months back—any idea who it was?"
"The Mex was one of 'em."

"What?" Ed exclaimed. "You talkin' about Armando Valencia—from down my way?"

"That's the one."

"We ran him out of town, Ken. Never figured he'd come north. He was always a desert man. Chased him all over Mojave a time or two—you remember those days for sure!"

"Well, he's on the move again now. That boy is always into somethin'. Got near ten thousand out of the bank here—lot of money, these days! He was ridin' with a few other ol' boys you might know—Riccardo San Dona and White Eyes Chapman."

"The wop and the half-breed? Never figured either one of those boys for banks! They do like to play poker, though. Chapman's a little handier at the game—plays big stakes. Must have run into some misfortune somewhere along the line. I wonder what they're doin' running with Valencia? Can't figure that one?"

"Nope, me neither," Ken Petty agreed.

San Dona had also worked as a lawman in southern California, but left law enforcement to pursue a job with an inventor, who was workin' on what they later called a *telephone.* Chapman on the other hand was a bounty hunter out of Pasadena, and had left town under a heavy cloud of false accusations surroundin' a dead cowboy he had brought into town, lyin' over a saddle and shot in the back. Caused Chapman his career as a bounty hunter, and he almost got hung, but lit out of town before an angry lynch mob could get holt of him.

"Had a man up the street as a lookout too—I can't be sure, but I think it was Harry Brown, from up Aurora way—that mining camp, just east over the border from Bodie."

"Harry Brown?" Ed shook his head in disbelief.

"I think so," Ken replied in a firm manner.

"Naw," Ed blurted. "Harry's a Nevada man. He never leaves Nevada—you know that. He owns silver mines in

53

Aurora. It don't make sense he'd be in on a bank robbery—runnin' with outlaws and such. I would just about swear he wasn't ridin' with them—maybe there's another reason he was here."

"Well, it was him, sure as shootin'. I know it sounds crazy," Ken continued, while Ed gave him a look that continued to signal some doubt. He caught the look.

"I know, Ed, it don't seem natural for a man of his fancy to be ridin' with the likes of Valencia. He must be broke, that's all I can figure. The price of silver is rock bottom right now, and some of the new folks arrivin' in town are from Aurora Nevada. They say the silver is runnin' out and the folks are leavin' town in droves. Some went west—to Bodie, but that's no place for decent folks."

"Well, I haven't heard anything about San Dona," Ed replied. "I still think he was crazy for givin' up bein' a lawman and chasin' after new fangled inventions. I had a run in with Chapman up in June Lake last year. He stole my horse and my good saddle—the one with the silver conches on it. Never did find him. He always was a good prankster. Can't figure him turnin' to bank robbing, though. He's more of a prankster than a robber, that's sure!

"As for Valencia, well, Ken, you know how slick he is at covering his tracks. He's been stealin' things all his life. He had a rough childhood and never got over it. Sometimes a man is forced into goin' one way or another, and Valencia got shoved around a lot as a kid. He was an orphan boy, you know—but he was a fast learner, no matter what he put his hand to, and he was a hard worker—got to admire him for that."

"Well, he's a lot slicker now," Ken replied. "He's hit near all the banks in northern California and some across into Nevada, I've heard, and vanishes each time without a trace. Now that I know Harry Brown *might* be running with them, I think I can put two and two together and understand why.

"Ed, you know how educated Harry is. You know he use to work for Wells Fargo. Put those facts together and I'd say he's probably the brains of the outfit. Valencia's not afraid of nuthin', that's why Brown took up with him—least ways best I can figger. As for Chapman, he's been driftin' up here now and again. He gets tired of Reno and comes to Bishop. Lots of big card games in Bishop. Pretty rowdy up there now, though—hard for a man to find a *quiet* game of poker.

"Like you, I still can't figure San Dona in with that group —but, then again, I'm not really sure why Chapman's goin' that route either—unless he lost his knack for card playin'."

"Well, there's quite a mixture of talent in that bunch, that's for sure," Ed replied. "Could make them hard to track. I still think you're wrong about Harry Brown. San Dona's a mystery too—just don't add up. Who's the US Marshal in this county?"

"Little Dave Swearengin."

"Lil' Dave? I swear—those boys are in for real trouble. He's the best lawman west of the Rockies, next to me—but I'm retired. And he can track anybody, over anything—day or night."

"Somebody comin' on up behind you," Ken motioned as he warned Ed. "A big fella, ridin' with a young girl. The ol' boy's wearin' a railroader's cap." The sheriff then began to chuckle a bit. "Might be a poker dealer, Ed—wearin' a change pot on his head. 'Bout all a hat like that's good for—except maybe for a chamber pot—heh heh. The man looks a bit ornery. Nice lookin' gal ridin' with him, though. She's a mite young for that ol' buzzard."

Looking up at Angel's Flight, above the Johnson Ranch

Into the High Country
Chapter 4

"**T**hey're friends of mine," Ed responded. "The girl is Jeremiah Johnson's niece."

"Holy…" Ken gasped. "Put my foot in my mouth again—I saw him a few weeks back. Spoke to him, I did. He said some of his family was comin' out. All the way from Ohio, he said. She's sure a pretty one. Her uncle's a rare breed, that's for sure. I've felt right proud to know him these last years."

Ed soon introduced both Carrie and Railroad Ron to the sheriff. "Railroad Ron?" he responded. "From over Denver way?"

Ron nodded his head in the affirmative.

"I swear," the sheriff exclaimed. "You're the fella what saved about fifty to sixty folks from burnin' to death in a railroad fire—passenger coach, I believe it was—least that's what the papers said. That train car ended up a just heap of ashes in the wind. You was a big hero in Denver—if that be you—was it?"

Ron nodded in the affirmative once again, to which the sheriff responded, "I swear! When I first laid eyes on you I figured you for a tinhorn—a mischievous one at that. Goes to show ya, looks are a mite deceivin'. I guess it was that change pot of a hat you're wearin'—throwed me off a bit."

Ron let out with a laugh. "I've worn this hat a long time, Sheriff Petty. Never could get use to a Stetson like you're wearin'. Mighty wide brim—can you see where you're walkin' in all that shade?"

Ol' Ken Petty chuckled a bit. "Naw—it's my big belly that keeps me from seein' where I'm walkin.' —Can I help you fine folks with anything today?"

He began to stroke the face of Railroad Ron's mount—figured he'd get the conversation movin' in another direction. He'd already put his foot in his mouth, and there was serious business at hand with the robbery havin' takin' place and all. We all get carried away at times with foolishness, and most of them times are at a time when we shouldn't.

Ed Shay then told him their reason for being in town had to do with pickin' up some supplies for their upcomin' journey. Told him a little bit about their plans as well. Sheriff Petty seemed a little concerned when they mentioned they would be headin' for Mineral King via the old Cottonwood Pass.

"Mineral King, eh? Well, there's gold all right, but I heard there was trouble over there—claim jumpers, murders and such. You boys ought not to go. Leave that young girl at Jeremiah's place and come join my posse. Bring Johnson with ya."

"You won't need a posse with Swearengin on their trail," Ed laughed. "And too much help can sometimes create problems—Lil' Dave travels light—you know that."

"I wouldn't be too sure," Ken warned. "If ol' Valencia and that bunch are goin' where I think they're goin', it'll take a hundred marshals to smoke 'em out. They'll be headed up to them crags above Horseshoe Meadow to hide out. You better tell Jeremiah to take the Onion Valley pass and not go through the Cottonwood area. That way you can bide some time.

"You're lucky he's goin' with you—because of that your chances of makin' it through without trouble just went from none to slim. You got to go through Horseshoe Meadow anyway, eventually—if you're goin' either way—and you could run smack into them boys. Yep, Cottonwood pass is trouble for sure. Best take Onion Valley—up above town here —over yonder way." Sheriff Petty pointed toward the mountain pass due north of the settlement.

"We'll let Jeremiah know, Ken. We might just bag those scoundrels for you," Ed laughed. "You know Johnson. He could sneak right up on those boys and capture them single-handed. I know he's gettin' older, but one look into his eyes and a man can see and feel that he ain't lost his touch. I for one would not want to tangle with him—and I'm a fair hand at tanglin'."

The sheriff just shook his head, a little disappointedly I might add, and waived good-bye at Ed, Ron, and Carrie as they rode off in the direction of the Big Pine General Store.

"You watch over them young'uns up there!" he yelled. "I'll let Little Dave know you're gonna' be up that way. Be a mighty big comfort to him knowin' Jeremiah Johnson is up in that pass—a *mighty* big comfort."

It didn't take long for the trio to find a few things at the general store. In those days it was one store that carried just about everything you would need and then some. Some of the smaller towns in the West still have 'em to this day. You can still buy about anything you need, and most of 'em have an assortment of novelties that you won't find anywhere else in the country.

Carrie got some candy and bought a little hand mirror for Hannah. She bought a unique handwritten book on mountain survival, and a leather bracelet made by the local Indians. Ed and Ron looked at about everything in the store and then picked up a few items as well.

They all got started back toward the ranch before dinnertime. Once they arrived, they passed on the news of the robbery at Big Pine to Jeremiah and Windwalker. After a fine supper they all went outside and sat on the porch, where they commenced to about it.

"There's no need to change our plans," Jeremiah encouraged. "I've learned not to worry in life. You step out each day to greet the sun and deal with things as they come. You've just got to roll with what's thrown at you. I don't know no other way anymore."

"You sound just like my dad," Carrie laughed. "He said you've learned most everything there is to know."

Jeremiah smiled at her words. "I wish that were true, Carrie. Fact is, I don't know much at all. But, I have learned to trust in God, that he'll provide what I need and provide it when I need it. Each day has its trouble, that's sure. Some days can be a mite worse than others.

"You just have to be patient enough to work through them. I'm not sure anyone is really in control of their destiny, and there are misfortune's along the way. You've got to learn to enjoy the good moments and learn to enjoy the challenges of the bad moments, and give thanks for both.

"It's a matter of balance. The animals know quite well how to do it. They've taught me much over the years. God put understanding in them just like he did us. We lost it somewhere along the line, and I swear—it's a never-ending struggle to get it back.

"To the animals, it's natural, because they know who made them. For us, we have trouble understanding because we allow other things to distract us. We forget who made us and allow our imaginations and emotions to rule us.

"We don't listen well to the wind, either. God speaks to us everyday through the things he's made. We don't hear him unless we're determined to know he's there—and that takes some learnin'."

"Your uncle is a wise man," Railroad Ron inserted.

"I know," Carrie replied. "I hope I can be like him."

"I don't think you should hope in that, my dear," Jeremiah responded with a laugh. "You just be who *you* are. God gives us each a purpose. We're as individual as those rocks on that mountain yonder," he gestured with a nod toward the boulder strewn, High Sierra escarpment, its mighty pinnacles appearin' as tall, dark sentinels under the shadows of dusk.

"Now, don't you forget that."

The next mornin' was indeed a busy one at the Johnson ranch. Long before daylight, David and Sheri Perez had brought their sons, one niece and a passel of nephews to the cabin, where they assisted in packin' gear and in makin' ready for their neighbor's journey. The couple also cooked a breakfast for that whole crew that mornin', and also insisted on cleanin' up in the cabin as well as the kitchen.

"Don't you worry, Jeremiah," Sheri Perez encouraged. "This cabin will stay nice and clean and cozy 'till you all get back. I made some jerky and some cookies, and they're in Marc's saddlebags, along with a couple medicine dressings in case someone gets hurt. Those dressings are laced with feather moss and mustard root—mind you throw a little water on them now and then to keep them damp."

"I'll do that," Johnson assured her. "And thanks for bringing your family up here to help out. It's mighty kind of you—nice to see all these young'uns."

"We're looking forward to Christmas with you," Sheri Perez said. "Along with this brood, we'll also have Ryan Running Horse, Cameron White Eagle, and Mason Kicking Bird—the boys from the Native American orphanage down in Lone Pine. We've been thinking about adopting them. Will your family be visiting for a while?"

"Well, they're my brother's children. He may let them stay a spell longer than planned. I was going to put them on a train after the holidays, but I like them being here. Maybe I can talk my brother into letting them stay a while longer—'till spring, maybe. Just might coax him into coming out here himself and make the whole thing a long-winded family affair."

By sunrise the group was well fed, saddled, loaded and ready. The weather above looked good—for now. There were no clouds on the peaks and warm air continued to prevail. Some snow was actually meltin' in the high country, which was somewhat unusual for December.

Jeremiah told the Perez folks not to worry, that they would only be gone about a week, and promised to bring them back an elk or two as part of their winter food supply. He said the elk could make a fine Christmas dinner.

"I got a few hogs," David Perez told Jeremiah. "We should be all right, senor—no need to go to any fuss for us."

Jeremiah patted him on the back. "I can't see a man livin' on hog when he can feed on elk," he said, as he climbed up into the saddle. "An old friend once told me that," he smiled.

"I'll be sure to find you some big elk. You take care now," he nodded, and then rode out and joined the others, who had ambled on down the road and were waitin' on him, expectin' that he would be the one to take the lead.

When they all got together and started on down the road toward the High Sierra Trail, Jeremiah, Hannah, Railroad Ron and Carrie rode abreast up front. My Dad and John Windwalker rode just behind them, while Ed Shay took up the rear, each of the latter pullin' a pack mule behind him.

The mornin' was exquisite. The sunrise was now in full bloom and castin' an orange glow on the eastern face of the Sierra. The air was full of the unmistakable scent of sage. A single hawk circled high above 'em, which Windwalker pointed out to be a very good sign.

"The hawk will guard us on our journey," he said. The young Marc (my Dad), riding abreast him, perked up his ears and was listenin' intently when Windwalker started talkin'— had an eye out on that hawk too. My Dad told me later that at his young age he was mighty proud to ride alongside

Windwalker and hear his words. He said he felt it was a great honor.

"The hawk will warn us if there is trouble, and he will alert us if there is any change in the weather. My grandfather taught me these things when I was very young. The creatures of the earth speak to us in many ways. I have learned to depend on their wisdom."

The seven riders soon turned west at a marked junction and headed up the High Sierra Trail through the Cottonwood Pass. The lower portion found 'em windin' through majestic stands of white and sugar (ponderosa) pine, with a few of the tall, western red cedar (redwoods) scattered here and there. There were sporadic hemlock and douglas fir—even a California black oak or two in the mix as well.

The narrow trail followed the high stream and some of the larger white granite boulders that dominate the eastern incline. That trail shifted periodically and directly paralleled the stream for a distance, then wound up through sporadic brush and still more pine, switchin' back and forth along the lower ridge, ascendin' toward the Mt. Whitney Portal. It was the younger folks first encounter with such virgin, awe-inspirin' beauty—nothin' like it back east where they come from.

They reached the first crest just before noon, and the view of the Owens valley from that point was indeed worth stoppin' to take a gander. From there the valley floor was close, perhaps three to four miles due east. The red rock boulders on the west side of that landscape were stacked tall enough, from that point, to obscure most of the valley floor itself, but the White Mountain range to the northeast could be seen in great detail.

From that lofty vantage John Windwalker pointed out a small herd of elk, just north of Lone Pine peak. He called the others attention to it, and all the riders reigned in and stopped for a spell.

"Elk are still up high this year. That means perhaps a mild winter, or a late one. If we spot any on higher up, then I'd say it's going to be a mild one. What do you think, Johnson?"

Jeremiah's eyes caught the elk, and then scanned the timberline on the peak above 'em.

"Some hawks on the higher pine up there—still nestin' I figure." He turned his eyes on Windwalker. "Mild winter, I'd say—least ways we can hope for it."

After a brief gander at the elk the riders hit the trail again, reachin' the timberline 'bout an hour later. Except for an occasional bray from the pack mules it was a quiet ride. They reached the first series of granite switchbacks a short time after that, some distance above the timberline.

The sun was at their backs and it was unusually warm at that higher elevation. Jeremiah slowed the pace of his horse and brushed at the animal's mane.

"We'll rest here a bit," he said. "Lot of work for these animals next mile or two."

The trail ahead was indeed steep as well as narrow, cuttin' back and forth sharply across a granite face, laid out with a series of a dozen or so switchbacks, barely three feet in width. The stretch between each switchback was a good fifty yards or more, and it always took some time to make the ascent.

"They call this place Angel's Flight," Jeremiah informed the riders. "You'll see why once we start up it. It's not near as bad as it looks, though, unless you're coming down at night. You can see sparks from the metal on shod horses, and you have to lean way back in the saddle. It gets a mite spooky. Goin' up ain't near bad, though.

"We'll go single file. John—you, Ron and Marc take the lead. We'll let the girls follow you and I'll get behind them. Ed, if you don't mind, I'd like you to take up the rear with the pack mules."

"I'll do that, Jeremiah," Ed nodded.

"Lean forward as you climb and give the horses all the reins," Jeremiah told 'em. "If you're brave, you can look down, otherwise keep your eyes straight ahead. Let the horses make the turns on their own. They know what they're doin' and they'll keep their own distance. It will look like a steep ascent from the saddle, but don't pay it no mind.

"We'll be up on top of this rock in a short time, and the trail will level off somewhat and head into a high meadow. We can rest again once we get there. Then we'll ride across to the west side of the meadow and camp for the night. It's a steep climb from there and it will take a good portion of the day tomorrow before we hit the high crest."

John Windwalker moved on up and led the ascent of the granite switchbacks. The riders trailed behind him at five to six foot intervals, and were lined up in their designated order as he reached the first turn. He looked below as he made the turn, checkin' on the younger riders, then again took sight on the trail ahead.

He made the next switchback turn soon, again checkin' the riders below him. My Dad told me that about that time he felt that the hair on his neck was standin' straight up.

"You're all looking good," Windwalker smiled. "Other than you youngling's faces bein' a mite pale on the turns, you're looking real good," he laughed.

"Marc, you grind on your teeth any harder, you're going to have a very sore jaw by the time we get up top."

My Dad looked up at him, then turned in the saddle to look at his younger sister, just behind him in the train. "You scared, Hannah?"

"Naw—this is fun," the girl smiled, lookin' round about her. She didn't look down, though, a sure sign that her words were more to encourage herself than to comfort her brother. "Don't you think it's fun?"

"I guess," my Dad replied.

65

With that, Jeremiah leaned forward in the saddle as he made the turn behind Carrie. "Hey, you kids best be glad it ain't dark. You'd be plenty scared, that's sure. When we come back, you best hope it's still daylight. It's spooky here at night —like I said earlier, you can see sparks flyin' off the horses' shoes."

"We ain't scared," my Dad blurted out.

"Liar liar, your pants are on fire," Hannah shouted at him.

"That's enough!" Carrie scolded, sternly yet softly. "You spook these horses and it could have serious consequences—so just think about that and shut up!"

"Well spoken," Railroad Ron added, looking straightway at the younger children. "Now ain't no time for mischief or actin' a' fool."

The younger riders then remained quiet for some time, until they were off of the switchbacks at Angel's Flight and had reached the first high meadow. Hannah rode up beside my Dad and apologized for makin' fun of him.

"I was just teasin'," she insisted. "Don't pay me no mind."

"I'll take it you meant it kindly," my Dad smiled. "I guess I *was* scared."

"We were all scared," Carrie added. "But, we made it!"

The lush meadow was a welcome site indeed. For nearly a mile square, bright green and yellow brush dominated the boulder-strewn landscape. A stream crossed the center of the meadow, droppin' down a bit at the first of many waterfalls, just north of the Angel's Flight ascent.

"We'll water here," Jeremiah said, bringin' his mount to a halt. "Best dismount and give the horses a rest. There's a camp just across the meadow. There's some firewood stacked over there, and stacked in a cave higher on up as well, compliments of a geological survey team that was up here nosin' around last year.

"We'll set up camp there at meadow's end, and I'll go fetch a few rabbits for dinner. We'll cook some beans, and there's some fruit in the supplies too. Got some sheepherder's bread packed in burlap—mighty good eatin'.

"John, let's go fetch some rabbits. The meadows full of them.

"Ron, after you all rest a bit, just head the group west across the meadow. You'll see the camp, just where the stream comes out of the rocks yonder at meadow's end. You and Ed get us a fire going and me and John will be back directly."

The trailside meadow is indeed a fine camp. In the summer there's a thick field of Indian paintbrush here (a most unique flower), splashed for two hundred yards across this carpet of sparklin' green meadow. A lot of manzanita grows here as well, with its glossy, leathery leaves and dark maroon bark. There are edible red-orange berries that grow on the plant, and they're a mite tasty.

One can become easily absorbed up here, studyin' the flowers and plants. Flowers and plants do have a distinct, individual appearance, but also much intricacy—somethin' we usually never notice or consider. My Dad taught me many things about the flowers and plants of the field. He said that both Windwalker and Jeremiah had inspired him to take a real close-up look at these kinds of things.

A few waterfalls dot the landscape up here also. Waterfalls can be experienced from below, from above, or from their sides with equal intensity. From below or from the side, one can watch individual spears of water, or comets some call 'em, slowly plunge downward, one row behind another, behind still another—all of 'em fallin' slower than the main mass of tumblin' water!

Endless water spears enjoy this few split seconds of individual identity before bein' reunited with the mass of water from which they first come. If there's a good wind, waterfalls may produce, either at the top of the fall or at the point of collision at the bottom, significant sprays. They're nice and cool on your face, after workin' up a sweat from ridin' all the way up the Flight.

Massive, graceful and captivatin'—specially if you can see 'em there within the sprays—are the rainbows, the colors of which are indescribable. By moonlight a waterfall is quite an admirable experience. The sprays appear as night specters, ridin' the wind. Wet rocks catchin' the moonlight shine like jewels, which in a short time disappear forever as the moon, ever changin' its angle, slips across the western sky.

The stream windin' across that meadow is a fine thing to sit beside at night and can be the most tranquilizin' of experiences. There's three small waterfalls, near the center of the meadow there, and each one is quite different from the others. You have to of course clear your mind of everyday things, and then, once you get some alertness about you, pick a spot where there's good movement of the water.

The younger folks—Carrie, my Dad, and Hannah, had found such a spot. The good ol' boys sharin' their adventure with 'em built a fire and began fixin' up some dinner over in the camp, just a short distance away. It was a teepee fire and a mighty fine one. Them boys was over there talkin' 'bout the good weather, the safe ride up the Flight, the terrain they would encounter come mornin', and so on.

There's some casual conversation among the younger folks as well. My aunt Carrie is leadin' the way. The girl was a teacher from her youth up. She knew somethin' about dang near everything. It was her gift. And she was patient in her teachin' as well—she had real style in the way she expressed things to folks, young or old—it didn't matter. She knew how to, shall I say, *season* her words? That paints the picture I believe. She retired from a teachin' career many years ago.

I swear—her students were dang lucky to have known her, those years she taught. I'm sure she inspired more than a few to carry on the tradition—least ways I hope she did. If they weren't inspired, well, they must have been danged ignorant is all I can figure.

Photo by Dan Campbell

The Outlaws!
Chapter 5

"**I** wanted to tell you both something I learned in school this year," Carrie began. "It's pretty clear out tonight, so when it gets real dark we ought to be able to see plenty of stars.

"The North Star is the most well known. It's not the biggest or the brightest, but what is really strange about it is that it doesn't seem to move like any of the other stars. All the other stars move across the night sky from east to west, and they change their positions with the seasons.

"The North Star is almost right above the North Pole. As the earth spins, that star remains right there in the northern sky. It's a real important star for navigation.

"'Navigation' is how you can find your way when you're lost. From any location on the earth above the 'equator'—that's the center of the earth—the angle of the North Star above the horizon gives you a 'latitude,' which is part of what you need to figure out where you are.

"Below the equator you can't see the North Star, so, you can't navigate by it down there. That's all I know about navigation, so far.

"They do say that birds use all the stars to navigate by. During their yearly 'migrations'—that's the directions they fly in when they go to and from a place—they appear to guide their flights by the many 'constellations'—constellations are big groups of stars—clusters of them."

"You're pretty smart, Carrie," Marc responded. "I know there's lots of stars, but I can't name any of them. How do you find the North Star anyhow?"

"That's easy," she replied. "You have to find the Big Dipper first—it's like the outline of a ladle. The two pointer stars at the very end of the cup point the way to the North Star.

You just count up five stars from the cup, and there it is! I'll show you in just a little bit," she said, as she kept an eye on the approachin' darkness.

"—And I'll teach you the names of some other stars too. We humans only know a few names, but God knows *all* their names. In fact, he named all the stars—did you know that?"

"Gosh!" Marc exclaimed. Little Hannah seemed equally surprised.

"Our sister knows lots of stuff," Hannah boasted. "You just ask her anything," she added, directin' her words at my Dad.

"Yeah?" he responded. "Well, how far is she gonna' jump when she sees that big snake that's crawlin' up behind her?"

"About ten feet!" Carrie barked, as she leaped immediately from the rock upon which she was sittin'.

"Just about that far!" she finished, as she landed feet first and rolled on into some brush nearby. That girl jumped near five feet in the air!

My dad was not joking—it was a snake all right, and they were for sure in rattlesnake country. Them rattlers can be mean critters. Fortunately for them it was only a gopher snake.

"I wasn't foolin'," my Dad said. "It's just a gopher, though —I'll go ahead and stomp on him."

"You'll do no such thing," Carrie warned. "He's just curious about us and isn't causing any trouble. He can hang around or do whatever he wants. What if you were him, Marc? Would you want some big ol' human to stomp on you?"

My dad developed a kind of sheepish look about himself. "No, I don't 'spect I would."

"Then why don't you escort our visitor back into the brush," Carrie suggested, as she stood up, dustin' herself off from her crude landin'. "Perhaps his family would appreciate it."

My Dad hesitated. "Well, maybe he's just out huntin' some food and don't want to go home just now."

"Snakes don't see well," Carrie replied. "The heat from our bodies may have him somewhat confused. I just think he may get his bearings back if you just put him over there in the brush —right over there."

My Dad moved slowly toward the snake and reached down, a bit hesitant to pick him up. At that moment Hannah gave a yell and at the same time, unbeknownst to the others, chucked a stone at my Dad, which struck him right square on the buttocks. "Lookout, Marc—there's another one right behind you!"

The boy just about jumped out of his skin as he reached around and grabbed hold of his butt—tryin' to figure out where he was bit. As it turned out there was no second snake, only laughter from Hanna and then from Carrie, after she seen that Hannah was just jokin'.

When my Dad caught on he scolded Hannah a bit, then scooped up the gopher snake and quickly carried it to some nearby brush—right where aunt Carrie suggested he be put.

A moment later the group could hear Ed Shay callin' out to them that chow was on. It didn't take long for them to skin out and shin for the campfire, where they commenced to dig into some fine trail food.

"You folks enjoying yourselves?" Jeremiah inquired of the youngsters. "I heard a bit of yelling and laughter from over there in the brush where you were."

"We were being educated," my Dad replied. "Carrie here seems to know a lot about the stars and such. We got a lesson in how to find the North Star. We had a gopher snake sneak up on us as well. I got a joke played on me and that was what most of the yellin' and laughter was all about."

"Snakes are plentiful up here. Rattler's mostly. You've got to be real careful," Jeremiah warned.

"I knew a fella once who got his ear cut off in an Indian fight. After things settled down a bit, one of the folks in our party sewed his ear back on. Trouble was, he sewed it on backwards. That fella heard a rattlesnake one evening, turned around to run away from it, and stepped smack into it."

"You're kidding, ain't ya?" Railroad Ron inquired, a bit of skepticism in his tone.

Jeremiah started to laugh and everyone joined in. "I didn't think any of you would fall for that," was his response. —"Anybody want some more food? Got another rabbit on the spit. If not, we'll use that critter to whip up some rabbit gravy for biscuits in the morning. I make fine biscuits and gravy."

It wasn't too long after that fine dinner that the entire group got a lesson in the stars from Carrie, and spent a bit of time gazing at them in the night sky. The stars seem so much closer from the mountains, and it's mighty dark up there too, which allows a lot more stars to become visible.

They each learned how to find the North Star that night, and could randomly identify some constellations as well— Aunt Carrie quizzed everyone on her lesson. Like I said, she was a fine teacher.

After a real interestin' evenin' they all bedded down for the night. It had been a hard day's ride and everyone was plum wore out. Most everybody slept sound. An owl could be heard now and then—up in a cedar tree not too far off.

An owl's hoot is a real song of the West—same thing goes for the wail of the coyote or the howl of the wolf—they make fine music. Those songs in the night are their way of lettin' you know that everything's alright.

Around midnight a wind begin to pick up from down below. Jeremiah was awakened by the sound of the lower elevation pines, creakin' and swayin' back and forth in the gale. Mountain winds can blow real strong at times—and there's no end to their howlin', due to 'em bouncin' back and forth from one slab of rock to another in such a rugged landscape. Each blast of wind seems to whistle a different tune.

Usually the wind stays along the lower escarpments, comin' in from the desert and all, but should the wind move up to their present elevation, well, there wasn't much protection in that meadow.

Winds comin' in from the desert got their own way. Sometimes they'll just blow on through and be gone, keepin' low, and at other times they'll hang around and start climbin' to the higher elevations, above the timberline. They get real mean up there, and they get cold—usually there's no place to hide from 'em, unless you know the mountain.

Jeremiah pondered whether or not he should rouse the others and move into the shelter of the granite crags just above 'em. Risky business, movin' at night, climbin' the mountain and all—especially with them younger folks in tow. The horses could spook real easy—yep, movin' was risky business at best. No tellin' what the wind might do—a mountain wind's got its own way—I said that before.

'I guess I'd better roust everybody up and get 'em movin' before that wind gets up here,' is what Jeremiah was a' thinkin' to himself.

There's a good lesson here. If you don't know a mountain —if you've never been there, then don't go up it when you know bad weather's a' comin'. If you have a choice, then wait out the bad weather—let it pass. Don't be a dang fool.

For Jeremiah there really wasn't much choice in the matter. Mountain winds can turn ugly most sudden like. But in this case things would most likely be all right—he knew the mountain. He knew of a real good sized cave in the crags up above—it was just a matter of gettin' everyone and the animals up and inside the shelter before any high winds reached their particular elevation.

Everybody rousted pretty easy, but then that's a natural thing in the mountains, with such fresh air and all. You can sleep well up there, but for some reason it's never a deep sleep. There's a natural alertness in the body, caused by the cleanliness of the air that one breathes in the high country— least that's what they say. Myself, I think it's because you're closer to God up there. Your body knows it, even if you don't.

They packed up quick. When all were mounted, Jeremiah took the point and guided everyone in haste out of the meadow and on up to a group of crags that marked an openin' into a fairly deep cave—near like a cavern—facin' the west slope.

The moonlight aided them for a while, but the clouds movin' in overshadowed that light in a hurry. They scrambled inside the cave with the horses in tow, and not a moment too soon. The storm rose up and hit with a fury.

It was impressively beautiful, though, the wind howlin' its tunes as it ascended the mountain, dancin' among great boulders and pushin' dark clouds along ahead of it. They all watched the gale intently from the mouth of the cave. It wasn't long before the rain began to move in. Thunder suddenly exploded among the clouds and the heavenly water came down in torrents.

That rap of thunder was followed in the wink of an eye by a nasty bolt of lightnin' that scared the daylights out of 'em, and forced 'em further on back into the cave's openin'. They say if you count the seconds between a rap of thunder and a bolt of lightnin', and then multiply that time by eleven-hundred feet per second, you can tell how far away the lightnin' is. Well, it was for sure right on top of 'em!

"How long you figure it will last, Jeremiah?" Ed Shay questioned.

"Hard tellin, Ed. I suggest you all better get some sleep, though. The going might be a little tougher, come morning. Trails don't take too kindly to rain—may wash them out a bit.

76

We'll be okay in here—I've never seen this cave fill with any run-off, and I've been coming up here for years."

Sleep did come to everyone after a little time of watchin' and listenin' to the rain. A heavy rain has a way of relaxin' the mind, then the body.

Far down below them, in the midst of that awful storm, some night riders were makin' their way up the mountain. There were three of 'em. They were soakin' wet, but mighty determined—none of their horses broke stride.

"We gotta' find some shelter, Armando," one of them blurted out to the lead rider. "Don't want all this money to get wet."

"There's a cave up yonder, wop," another spoke.

It was the half-breed, White Eyes Chapman. "We'll be up there directly and outa' this weather. I told you to throw a blanket across them saddle bags a while back. You knowed it was gonna' rain. I swear—it's hard to figger out just how a wop's a' thinkin' sometimes."

"S'pose that lawman's following us?"

It was Riccardo San Dona, the third rider—a man of Italian descent—who posed the question. He knew that Chapman had a dislike for Italian folk. Fact is, he didn't take to foreigners of any kind—even the Mexican, but he was ridin' with 'em. More than likely it was his own self that he didn't like. That's usually the seed at the core in the rotten apple of prejudice. Name-callin' didn't bother San Dona none, though. He was a man that didn't rile easy, and he knew Chapman—knew that he was just wind, mostly.

Armando Valencia looked back at him through the rain. "I don't see nobody or hear nobody, amigo. Besides, Lil' Dave Swearengin ain't nobody anyway. You can take him, Ricky-boy, I'm sure. He's fast, amigo, but I hear you're faster."

"Do tell," San Dona answered. "But I'm not gonna' draw on no lawman. You give me my share and I'll ride on. I'm not planning on meeting up with Swearengin. I have nothing against the law, as I use to be a lawman. I have no idea what I'm even doing here! Lil' Dave was my friend—at one time."

"You ain't got no good friends no more, amigo, and we'll do the split when we get to the cave," Armando Valencia barked.

"Fact is, you ran out on your friends, thinkin' you'd be Mr. Genius, with that new fangled telephone company. That didn't work out, and neither did that job you had in Barstow, so you joined on up with us. I'm not sure we're your friends either— can't trust no former lawman. Besides, it was me and Chapman that done the hold-up, amigo. You stood outside, remember? I let you ride out now, you just might run to Swearengin and tell him where we're at."

"He ain't gonna' tell Swearengin," Chapman scowled. "I've known him a while, and he's always been a man of his word—even though he's a wop. That's why I brought him in on this caper. He's my friend, wop or no, and if you ride him too hard, Armando, you'll be dust in the wind come spring, cause I'm a better gunman than both of ya."

"Well, don't wet your pants," Valencia growled. "Cave is just ahead there—rainin' harder now too, and gettin' dang cold —might snow! You gringos best kick up your horses and move on—de prisa! It's difficult to hear anyone comin' up on us if we keep on a' jawin' like this. So don't talk—just ride."

With heavy cloud cover veilin' the moonlight, the mouth of the high cave was barely visible through the downpour of rain. Hunkered in their saddles the riders pushed on and didn't talk none. The trail was somewhat covered in water runoff, causin' the horses to be a little apprehensive of the climb. A sudden flash of lightnin' revealed the natural shelter in the higher rocks above. It wasn't too far off now. The three riders spurred on against the runoff, makin' their way toward it.

Meanwhile, Windwalker moved to waken Jeremiah when he heard them a' comin'. I don't know how he heard them in all that rain, but you've got to be an Indian to know those things. He judged the riders were still a good three hundred yards or so away. He took a' hold of Jeremiah's shoulder and spoke quietly in the darkness.

"Riders—Wahseechu—three, maybe more. Might not be friendly—better get ready, Johnson."

Jeremiah was up in a heartbeat. "Let's get everyone into the back of the cave. Whoever they are they won't be able to see us in this darkness. Be quick about it, John!"

The two of them rousted out the others and the movement of everyone was indeed hasty. Windwalker put a finger to his lips, insistin' they all move around as quietly as possible, so as not to spook the horses.

"What *about* the horses?" Carrie whispered. "What if they *do* make noise?"

"They're trained good," Jeremiah assured her. "Trust me. You and Marc get on back a' ways and keep Hannah close by. Hunker down there among the horses and nobody makes a peep—got it?"

"We can handle that," my Dad answered. "You heard him," he whispered boldly to his sisters. "Nobody makes a peep."

After movin' the animals and seein' the youngsters to their place, Jeremiah returned to the front of the cave where Windwalker was crouched down, peerin' out into the rain.

"Where are they, John?" he whispered. Ed Shay and Railroad Ron approached quietly and knelt down beside them.

"Not far—two hundred yards out, maybe. They're moving real slow—like molasses in the wintertime. A bit slick under those horses' hooves. They're a mite skittish about the climb.

The riders cut them no slack—they should be dismounting and leading the animals up here.

"These men are like the desert drought—I do not like the character of these men. There are three riders for sure—could be those bank robbers—the ones out of Big Pine."

Slowly, silently, Windwalker cocked the saddle rifle in his hands. "Got any ideas, Johnson?"

Jeremiah squinted to see through the rain, but couldn't get a line of sight on the approachin' riders. He then looked at Windwalker and the other men crouched beside him.

"They know the cave is here, and I 'spect they're planning on waiting out the storm inside. If there are only three of them, we can take them after they settle in. Let's all go to the back of the cave and lay low with the horses and the young'uns. We'll spread out so we won't be side by side if they start shooting. Maybe they'll go to sleep before too long. If they do, we've got 'em sure. We'll just have to play it by ear. Let's go—John, keep an eye here until you have to move."

John Windwalker nodded. "Go ahead—I will come back directly."

The three men moved into the back of the cave and fanned out, takin' prone positions on the rock floor amongst the horses. They checked their firearms and made ready, then holstered 'em again. Jeremiah glanced back to see the younger folks, huddled he hoped, at the rear of the cave, but it was too dark to see anyone. The horses were real quiet too.

'I guess we're as ready as we'll ever be,' He thought to himself.

Outside, the riders were now just about a hundred yards off. Valencia was in the lead, followed by White Eyes Chapman, while San Dona brought up the rear.

"Ain't too far now," Valencia yelled back at the others. "Gonna' be a lot dryer real quick, amigos!"

Windwalker watched as the riders neared the entrance to the cave. A sudden flash of lightnin' allowed him to see 'em real good. He recognized White Eyes Chapman right off—from the old days. His experiences with him had never been pleasant. Yet, his thoughts were merciful toward the man; He knew Chapman was a product of the white men's greed. Raised in a prejudiced environment, his Native American mother and white father were killed by hooded white men. Chapman had later embarked on a life ruled by what Windwalker called 'the dark side.'

He rode against him in two of the late Indian wars. Windwalker could have killed him on both occasions, but figured the spirits wouldn't deal too kindly with him had he done so—White Eyes bein' a half-breed and all. There was also a good side to Chapman, a spark that Windwalker's association with him over the years followin' the Indian wars had failed to ignite. Perhaps this present meetin' might bring things to a head—perhaps matters would be ironed out, or forever settled.

Windwalker moved quietly to the rear of the cave as the riders entered. They ducked in under the entrance one at a time and dismounted, glad to be in out of the rain, and led their animals a bit further on into the shelter. They didn't bother takin' off the saddles, though, just pulled off the bedrolls and the saddlebags. Windwalker was right. Them boys weren't to partial to their animals. Hard livin' can do that to folks—sear natural affection with a hot iron.

"I'll build a fire," Valencia said. "Maybe we can dry out a bit. It's darker than sin in here. I know this cave goes back a long way—cavernoso—but we best stay up front here and stay alert."

"I hope this storm passes by quick," Chapman growled. "Get that money out, Riccardo, and let's get it split up. I got some ridin' to do myself. I want to get out of these mountains

81

and head for Arizona. Weather's nice and folks are plum cordial down that way. You boys are dang fools for hangin' out up here. An Indian tried to set me straight down there years ago —should have listened to him. Now, I'm runnin' from the law in bad weather—no tellin' where I'll end up."

"We go where the money is, Chapman," Valencia barked. "You're thinkin' strange all of a sudden, and I don't like it— Gringo! You saddled this bronc, along with us, and I figure you better ride it—so quit complainin'. You best quit jawin' and help me find some firewood so's we can see in the dark. I don't figure you'll get a fair count if San Dona can't see what he's countin'."

"Ain't no dry wood here a'bout's," Chapman responded. "I say we just get some sleep until mornin'. Lord knows we're all dead tired and not in the best of moods. Let's just let things be 'till then. A man don't think well or say the best things when he's tired, nor when he's hungry, and most certain when he ain't had no sleep. So let's undo them bedrolls and get that sleep. Ain't nobody gonna' bother us here, nor track us in all this rain."

"I'm gonna' go to sleep all right, as I 'spect San Dona here is as well," Valencia growled. "But, you ain't lord of the manner here, White Eyes. If you think you are, just go for your gun, amigo. I'll bury you here."

"I swear, you boys are jumpier than two grasshoppers in a hot griddle," San Dona spoke up. "I'm beddin' down. Now lets hear no more talk about foolishness. None of your talk makes sense anyway. Chapman's right. We're too tired to build a fire, and too miserable to enjoy it. We'll count this money at first light—that's soon enough—can't see what I'm countin' in the dark anyway. We got plenty of time. The rain will wash out our tracks—all the way down the mountain. Nobody is gonna' find us here."

Chapman eyed Valencia. He was so fixed on him that I don't figure he heard a word San Dona had said—that's what my Dad told me, anyway. Anger was just boilin' out of the man's ears.

"You ain't gonna' bury nobody, Armando. You ain't quick enough to drop the hammer on me, boy. You won't even clear leather."

Chapman started for his gun, but hesitated when his hand touched the gun butt, as Valencia had already cleared leather and had the drop on him. A sudden blast of lightnin' just outside revealed that to Chapman—vividly, and it informed Valencia that the man hadn't yet pulled iron, and no longer intended to—spooked 'em both a little bit.

I say the good Lord saved Chapman at that very moment when the lightnin' spoke. And he saved Armando Valencia from a downright senseless shootin'. Things happen for a reason, you can count on that.[1] I've lived too long not to think otherwise.

Photo by Dan Campbell

A Christmas Miracle
Chapter 6

Valencia had drawn and cocked that ivory handled, blue steel Colt so fast that the others never even saw him move. As that flash of lightnin' danced across the sky, he glanced over at San Dona and then looked back at Chapman, who backed off and raised his hands in a gesture of submission. Armando Valencia then uncocked his piece and holstered it.

"Well, now I *am* gettin' a little jumpy—tired, I guess. Good night then," he spoke softly through a firm grit of his teeth.

The other two outlaws breathed a sigh of relief and all was quiet. Within a few minutes each of them had found a place on the floor, just inside the cave's entrance. Before long they drifted off to sleep. They were plum wore out. Their mounts stood against the wall of the cave for a time, but soon found comfort on the floor as well. The rain continued heavily outside, but no more lightnin' flashed that night.

Windwalker, Johnson, Railroad Ron and Ed Shay had maintained their place and were still awake in the back of the cave. The younger folks had nodded off shortly after the strangers had bedded down. As the three intruders began to breathe heavily, Johnson crawled quietly over to Ed Shay's position

"What do you think, Ed," he whispered. "You're and ex-lawman—what now?"

"One thing sure," Ed replied softly, "They underestimate Lil' Dave Swearengin. He can track anybody—over any thing, day or night, and rain don't matter. I'd say he's on his way up here, and I'd say we can count on that in doing whatever it is that we have to do.

"I think we should wait until first light. We can give them a wake up call, tie them up, and hold them for Lil' Dave and his posse. I can ride back down and fetch Dave up a little faster, if you'd like."

Jeremiah thought on Ed's words for a few moments. "Sounds good, but I don't want to risk waking them up by you sneakin' on around them. Can't count on your horse being real quiet—might stir up their horses. We'll just have to hope Lil' Dave is on his way. From what I've heard, you're right—he's got a gift for tracking. Best white tracker in these parts, they say—tracked Apache during the Indian wars, out in Arizona.

"The army always swore up and down that it takes an Apache to track an Apache. It's my understanding they sang a different tune after they hired Lil' Dave. —I'll stand first watch and you and the others can get some sleep. The last man on watch can wake the rest of us prior to first light. There's four of us and three of them, and we've got the edge in a surprise wake up. Shouldn't be any trouble—go ahead and get some sleep. I'll inform the others."

The night passed quickly. Just before dawn, Jeremiah and the others quietly surrounded the outlaws as they slept. They waited, they watched. Armando Valencia was the first to stir. Windwalker spoke to him from the shadows. The rain continued heavily outside.

"Hombre! Don't twitch a finger or move a muscle. I'm an Indian and your scalp looks mighty good. If you don't do exactly as I say, it's sure to be hanging from my lodge pole. You remember what the Apaches did to your people south of the border? Down in Nogales? I'm sure you don't want history to repeat itself here. Now—get up slow and quiet, and back up towards my voice, or I'll drop this hammer."

"What do you want, amigo—the money?" Valencia snarled, as he rose and backed up slowly, his hands raised in the air, toward the directin' voice of Windwalker, from somewhere in the darkness of the cave.

"The money doesn't belong to us," Windwalker responded. "It belongs to those settlers down in Big Pine. You will take it back to them. Now, get down on your belly and put your hands behind your back." While he spoke the other intruders awakened.

"The rest of you cowboys do the same, or I will have many scalps—the Indian way. The old days are gone, but I have not forgotten how to take a scalp."

"I know this Indian," Chapman breathed. "Can't see him well in the dark, but his voice is real familiar. He never lies—best do as he says."

The three outlaws had no choice. Surrounded by Jeremiah and company, guns leveled at them, they complied with the firm voice of the Indian, John Windwalker. Ed Shay and Railroad Ron hastened to bind up their hands and arms, and then directed them to sit up abreast of one another in the center of the cave. The outlaw's weapons were confiscated.

There was plenty of firewood in the rear of the cave, left there by a geological survey crew, just as Jeremiah had said. It was a mite cold, so he constructed a teepee style campfire, which lit up the front portion of the cave in a fine fashion. They could feel its warmth right off.

Carrie and the other children soon emerged from the rear of the cave, into the light and the warmth, to have a closer look at the intruders. The outlaws looked up at the youngsters but said nothing. After a brief time of studyin' each one of 'em, Carrie spoke out boldly at 'em.

"You men ought to be ashamed of yourselves for taking all that money. What if some young baby needed milk and all their parents had was saved up in that bank? What if a part of it was some old folks' life savings?

"How can you be so selfish as to think you could steal from other people—especially at Christmas time? Why don't you all get a job if you need money? My uncle has lots of jobs on his ranch—don't you, Uncle Jeremiah?"

She looked over at Jeremiah in the fire's light, who remained silent as she continued. "My dad always said, 'if a man doesn't work he shouldn't eat.' Now, we're going to have some breakfast pretty soon, and I am sure you are hungry, and I will see that each of you get some food, *if* you promise to quit this life of stealing, believe in God and Christmas, and go to work."

The outlaw Chapman looked at the girl as she stood near the fire in the dimly lit cave, his eyes reflectin' admiration and respect, his voice, kindness; "I don't think it's gonna' be as easy as all that, young lady. I figure the three of us here will have to spend some time in jail before we can go to work."

The other two bound outlaws laughed at that remark. All of their eyes were now on Carrie, each of them curiously impressed with her boldness.

"Yer like that flame of fire there, girl," White Eyes Chapman spoke out. "Are you a flame of hope for some old, worn out men of ill repute? Besides, I don't think your uncle there would really give us a job, now, do you?"

Carrie looked at her uncle, waiting for him to respond in some way. He thought on it for several moments, searchin' for the right way in which to answer. He looked back at her, knowin' she needed somethin' to go on—somethin' to encourage a young girl's hopes. She sure was of the forgivin' sort—a rare thing, he thought. But he was pleased with her attitude—it seemed to warm him inside. He then turned his attention toward Chapman and the others.

"I always have jobs at the ranch. Whether a man's ridin' a grub line or looking for a job, I never refuse him either one. Winters are a little slow, but if a man is willing to pull his weight and he's got his mind right, I'll hire him. If he can't stand up to the work, I'll give him three days grub and a head start.

"Now, if you boys were to turn in that money voluntarily, the law might go easy on you up here. Least ways, I haven't seen any wanted posters on you boys for anything else, though I've heard plenty about each one of you.

"But, I never judge a man by what others say about him. A man can change from one day to the next—I've seen it happen. Sometimes a man will go bad because he can't find a reason to do good. Once he finds a reason to do good, he doesn't think of goin' bad anymore. I guess it's the luck of the draw mostly, and I figure a lot of it has to do with being in the right place at the right time.

"But, some men try to do right no matter what. Others do wrong no matter what. Each man has a choice in this life. Best make the most of your choices when you have them." He looked back at Carrie momentarily, who was looking directly at him. Her eyes sparkled with admiration. He must have said the right things. He then returned his attention to the outlaws. "I'd say you boys have a choice right now."

"That's real fine, senor, but I don't figure the law is gonna' be as forgiving as you think." It was Armando Valencia who spoke out. "They're gonna' know we didn't volunteer nuthin', bein' as we're tied up like this, senor."

"You don't have to stay tied up," Jeremiah responded. "You can give your word that you won't run off, and we can tell the marshal when he gets here that we were just about to go back to town with you so you could turn yourselves in. We could tell him we were helping to provide an escort for the money. Lil' Dave will believe me when I tell him that, because I wouldn't be lying. Never met him personally, but I hear he's a fair man. He'll trust me—my word is good in these parts, and I'm sure he knows that. How's yours?"

"Why would you do that for us?" San Dona questioned. "You don't owe us anything. We don't even know you."

Railroad Ron spoke out: "His name's Johnson. Jeremiah Johnson."

The outlaw's eyes all turned toward Jeremiah. White Eyes Chapman was the first to speak.

"So you're him...him. They call you the *Spirit Warrior* back in Colorado. Apaches down Arizona way know about you too. Legends say it was an honor just to see ya, let alone talk firsthand with ya. I know your friend there—Windwalker. He helped me a time or two back in the old days. He spoke of you, but to most of us in those days you *were* just a legend."

"Well, the legend's right smack in front of you now," Ron blurted. "The bright young girl is his niece. A bit spirited, ain't she? Wisest young lady I ever heard talk as well. Takes after the old man, here. Now, the way I see it, he's offered you boys somethin'—legend or no."

All was quiet in the cave—if it wasn't for the cracklin' of the fire, you could most likely hear a pin drop. Jeremiah looked at his niece. "You have anything more to say, Carrie?"

"Yes, I do."

"Go ahead then."

She looked at the outlaws, still bound on the floor of the cave, side by side next to the fire. "I believe that people can change if they really want to. I believe it's up to us, as God's children, to support them when they do. Trust is something that is pretty rare. Now, if you give back that money, you've started to build some trust.

"It's up to the rest of us forgive you. As far as I'm concerned personally, though we'll have to wait on the marshal —to see what he thinks, you can walk out of this cave as free men with that foundation—the foundation of forgiveness. From there you can either build on it, or tear it down again. You

90

make a choice everyday in this life. You choose, from day to day, who you want to be.

"Lord knows we have opportunity to do whatever and be whatever we want," she smiled. "That's the hard part of life—choosing to be who you should be. It's easy to do wrong and hard to do right—for any of us. But, you've got to live with yourself, and you've got to live in a world with others around you. So that makes your choices real important. My dad taught me these things. I'm young and haven't made a lot of choices, but I know not to choose the way you've chosen.

"The choice you men made back in that town hurt a lot of people. Nobody was physically hurt, so you have a chance to make it right. If someone would have been physically hurt, then you would have to live with that. That's how things pile up in life and make it hard to change your ways. You sort of become what you've done. It's a terrible trap. If you keep doing bad things, it's hard *not* to do bad things.

"But, God gives us a freedom that no one else can give us. He forgives the worst of us, and sometimes that makes the best of us. So, you have a choice. I don't know if that marshal will think like this—"

Carrie looked back at Jeremiah, anticipating that he would say something at this point. He remained silent. "You should pray that the marshal is a just and a kind man," she continued. "He might be fair with you—being that it's Christmas and all. That's all I have to say, Uncle Jeremiah—except, I just realized how much I love my dad—your brother."

Johnson stood up and walked over to Carrie. Putting an arm around her, he said, "Gideon's a fine man—a good man—She's right boys—you do have a choice. Like I said, you best make the most of it."

Armando Valencia was the first of the outlaws to speak out in reply. "We'll give back the money, senor—right amigos?"

The others answered him affirmatively and nodded in agreement.

"Lil' Dave Swearengin's going to have some questions for you and your amigos," Jeremiah warned.

"Yeah, like where's Harry Brown?" Ed Shay blurted.

Valencia looked at the other outlaws, who appeared somewhat puzzled. "Senor, we don't know any Harry Brown," he responded.

"He's a fancy dresser from Nevada," Ed continued. "Always wears a long coat and a top hat—owns some silver mines up that way. He use to work for Wells Fargo."

"That don't bring nobody to mind," Valencia answered.

"I know who you're talkin' about now," San Dona interrupted. "He still works for Wells Fargo. He's like a secret agent type of guy. I never met him, but heard of him up Reno way. He's got a partner named West—Jim West, I think. They've got their own train—investigate robberies and such all over the west—even in the east. They're tough men."

San Dona stopped to think for a moment. "There's a third fella who runs with 'em too—Arte—somethin? —Artemus Gordon, that's it! He's clever, that Gordon—good at disguisin' himself. Catches a lot of outlaws that way."

"Well, Harry Brown was seen in Big Pine when you boys hit the bank," Ed responded. "And as for you, Riccardo, you worked with me as a lawman years ago. I don't understand you livin' this way now—not at all. Chapman there has always been a drifter, but I never figured him for robbin' banks either."

San Dona lowered his head for a brief moment. "Well, that telephone inventor that I had gone to work for wasn't too bright. I showed him how to make it work, but when the product started to sell, he fired me—didn't want to share any of the profits. I took to driftin' after that and ended up in Barstow. Took a job in a print shop. I invented a little machine I called a 'typewriter'—you know me, always tinkering—but the shop owner got a patent on it and booted me out.

"I was a two-time loser. Perhaps a three-time loser after that—I ran into Chapman there in the local tavern. We took to huntin' beaver. He had to quit bounty huntin' after that back shootin' incident. But, ornery as he is and as foolish as I was for running with him, I know he never shot that fellow in the back—found him that way in the brush—ain't that right, White Eyes?"

Chapman nodded in agreement. "I never shot nobody I didn't have to—and I never shot no one in the back! Got railroaded by some fancy lawyer—then that dang lynch mob come at me and I lit out. Their guns was a' blazin that day, but them boys was poor shots. They must have all been married men who loved their families, 'cause when I started shootin' back at 'em, they scattered and run for home."

"Anyway," San Dona continued, "we hunted beaver up in the White Mountains that winter—me and Chapman. Over a mile long, that string of beaver pelts—had to tie 'em tail to tail just to drag 'em down the mountain. The money didn't last long, though, so we took up with Valencia over in Modesto. We hit some Wells Fargo banks in Sacramento, Auburn and Reno—something I wish we'd never done."

"And Harry Brown took up the chase." Ed Shay interrupted. "That's probably why he was in Big Pine. Odds are he'll be ridin' with Lil' Dave Swearengin, and they'll show up here—sure as shootin'."

"Untie them," Jeremiah ordered.

Railroad Ron and Ed Shay moved quickly to loosen the ropes on the captives. Valencia then spoke up.

"Thank you, senor. —I been a bad seed all my life. Never heard nobody talk like this young senorita. My madre died when I was just a younker, so I never had no learnin' in what was right. Never knew no God, and never had no Christmas—

no las Navidades. I've lived by the feud—by the gun near all my life—pistolero. Never seen nobody care like this niece of yours, Johnson—never heard such words. Who is these other children?"

"The boy is my nephew, Marc. The younger girl is Hannah. These are Carrie's brother and sister. Their dad's back east—Carrie mentioned him—my one and only brother, Gideon."

Valencia gestured warmly with a nod at the children. "The three of us have heard of your uncle. Who hasn't in these parts?

"You're a mountain man, Johnson—a rare breed—like the blanco lobo—the white wolf. I never figured you for a family man. Your reputation makes you out a tough hombre—a loner, and you live like a wisp of smoke, roamin' the high country. This ain't no place for a family man—it is unruly here and wild —desenfrenado! Comprende?"

Jeremiah looked into Valencia's eyes. "I understand. But time changes a man. Relationships change a man—where he lives doesn't matter. I've been allowed to live two lives—the one I learned with, and the one I've lived with after that.

"The Creator's been kind to me—his Spirit, merciful. I've learned to walk with my head bowed. Gentleness, kindness and peace are my companions. My worst enemy taught me these things. His son is my partner—the Indian here is John Windwalker, son of a great Crow chief named Paints-His-Shirt-Red."

Windwalker looked at the three men and their eyes met his. He was a fierce lookin' man—I mentioned that earlier—his face bore the scars of many battles and his eyes appeared to look into men's souls, yet there was a distinct spark of compassion in them as well. His captives—especially Chapman, knowin' Windwalker personally, could feel this compassion and spoke directly at him.

94

"Your eyes have seen much, I'm sure. You are a great warrior. I was with you in all that blood and guts durin' the late wars. We've both been warriors in a different way, but we seek peace in our hearts. I speak for Valencia and San Dona as well. It is an honor to meet a warrior like you in the struggle of life —to look into your eyes and see both war and peace—both death and life.

"I saw that years ago and I see it now—but I was a wandrin' fool in them days and went my own way. Again, like I said, the three of us also seek peace, but struggle within to find it. How did a man like yourself find it—after all that you've seen and been a part of? I swear—I can't figure that out. My head is in a spin tryin' to understand it."

Windwalker squatted down by the fire, still eyin' the three men. "There is only one God, both for the whites and the Indian—for the Spaniard also—for all men. My father knew of this God, as does Johnson. He made all things in this life, and if a man seeks him with his eyes and his ears, in all the things that are made, then his heart will be filled with him. Then there is peace—a peace that comes to rule in ones life. Wisdom then becomes his counselor, and he can live with himself and with others. Men are no longer his enemies in his heart."

Windwalker paused for a moment to gather his thoughts, while placin' a little more wood on the fire. Them outlaws was thinkin' mighty hard on everything he was sayin', and never once interrupted him. It was like their lives had all of a sudden come to a halt—slowed down so's they could begin to get a good look at what was on the inside. Presently, Windwalker finished what he had to say.

"If you want to free yourself from the storms that rage in your heart, then you must seek this peace. Only the Great Spirit can give it to you—otherwise, you will carry your rage within to your death—and beyond. You will destroy yourself through the hardness of your own heart—and the fire will not be

95

quenched. I am honored to have learned these things, as is Johnson, who knows of these things as well. It is a great honor to teach you men of them."

As Windwalker was speaking those last few words the three men began to weep. And when they looked across the fire at Windwalker, there was a sparkle in their eyes that my Dad said he never forgot. He said there was all of a sudden a 'strange glow' from that campfire, which lit up those men's eyes for just a few moments—then it was gone—the fire was 'natural' again.

Everyone in the cave was astounded when that happened. They all looked at one another when they seen them men's eyes light up like they did. Even their faces glowed for a brief moment and you could see the tears on their cheeks. My Dad said he thought that angels must have reached out from the fire and touched them. He cried when he told me about it. My Dad was always tender in heart when he talked about God and angels. I always respected him for that.

Jeremiah later told my Dad that them boys had been 'truly humbled.' He said he saw it in their eyes. He said that only God could humble men like that, and that it was mighty rare that he allowed it. He said that God loved a broken spirit—a contrite heart—a deep sorrow for sin and its consequences. He was glad that my Dad got to witness it—said it was a 'divine occasion.' Jeremiah also said he'd never seen nothin' like it before—never even heard of it happenin' like that.

Windwalker later told my Dad it was the eyes of the Great Spirit looking into the eyes of those men—right outta' that fire! He said that God had heard them weeping, and came to encourage them. He said that he had seen it once before—long ago when his father returned from his last battle with Johnson. He said it happened at the council fire, when his father wept and said that he had forgiven Jeremiah for his sins against the

Crow Nation. Windwalker also said that he'd never told Jeremiah about that, but figured it was time to do so.

Nobody inside the granite walls of that cave said anything after that strange event took place. All you could hear for a spell was the cracklin' of the campfire that they were all sittin' around, and the sound of the heavy downpour of rain just outside the cave. The light of day was just beginnin' to filter in through the rain.

Cottonwood Pass, south of Mt. Whitney

The Wisdom of the Mountain Man
Chapter 7

John Windwalker suddenly stood to his feet. "Horses approaching in the rain. Not far away now—two, maybe three riders, from the southeast—they have come up through Cottonwood Pass."

"Most likely Lil' Dave Swearengin, I 'spect," Ed Shay spoke out. "Let's hope we can get him in on this conversation."

The riders came to a halt near the entrance of the cave and dismounted. Muffled voices were soon heard outside, talkin' with one another through the rain. One man then yelled out in the direction of the cave's entrance, and no one had any trouble hearin' what he said.

"You in the cave—come out with your hands empty, or else be ready to meet your maker! Name's Swearengin, US Marshal. I deal in lead, and I'm a good shot—hit what I'm aimin' at—even in the heavy rain, so don't be fools. You'd better move!"

The voice *was* that of Swearengin. Shay recognized it right off. He then responded, shouting out from within the entrance.

"Come on in out'a all that rain, Lil' Dave. Ain't no guns pointed at you. It's Ed Shay, from down Los Angeles way. I Got Jeremiah Johnson in here with me, along with a friendly Indian and an ol' railroader, and them three fellas you're lookin' for. There's some young'uns in here too, so be careful with your guns!"

"Shay? —I swear, if that don't beat all—we're comin' in— guns ready, though, until we're sure! You'd best be Shay, or you can count on gettin' shot."

Dave Swearengin moved cautiously into the cave totin' a Winchester rifle, cocked and ready. Harry Brown was just behind him with a cocked peacemaker in each hand. The third

99

man in was no stranger to Shay. He had a nickel-plated pistol shoved into a waistband and another in a shoulder holster, pearly white grips mounted on both of 'em—fine lookin' pieces. His right hand was up and ready to pull on the shoulder piece, and there was a heap of confidence in his manner.

It was Doctor Steven Gilmore, a retired physician turned deputy US Marshal. Most knew him as the gun totin' doctor, but just called him 'Doc.' He was good with a gun—fast and deadly accurate, but known to pull a cork now and then and chase the women, which went against his oath as a member of the medical profession.

You could count on him, though, when he was sober, that's for sure. Lil' Dave wouldn't take him along if he was drunk. When he needed him, he'd just throw him in a horse trough and dunk him a time or two to sober him up.

It's sad to see a medical man be like that, but no one knew what made him that way and he never talked about it. He come from Virginia, but no one really knew much about his life back there, and no one dared ask him—that's just the way things was. We all got our skeletons. Most of us just don't want to dig 'em up.

But, my Dad taught me that it was good to dig up them ol' bones now and then. He said that holdin' things in will cause all kinds of problems in one's life. He said you had to resurrect them ol' memories and let those things vent, and if you did, you would find out that other folks have gone through dang near the same things—maybe even worse!

He said that once you find that out, things don't seem so bad, and you can begin to heal from all them wounds that you carry. Life can have some purpose again. He said you could never even hope to shed any light on your purpose without the wounds. Wounds was a necessity, he said. And you had to talk about 'em with someone else, or there would be no healin'. Not a chance!

"I see you got the Doc ridin' with you, Lil' Dave," Shay said. "That was a wise choice—nobody's gonna' pull against him."

"You bet! Big reward in this capture—offered by this Wells Fargo man, Harry Brown. Doc stays sober when money's involved—becomes downright useful to me!"

Swearengin then looked at the three captives seated at the fire. "Why ain't these men tied up, Shay?" He quickly moved his rifle barrel toward them.

Shay looked at Johnson and Windwalker, then at Railroad Ron and the children. Seeing the man's hesitation, Jeremiah spoke up.

"I'm Johnson. These men are, well, sort of in my custody—under my trust, you might say. Put the guns down and let's talk about them."

Lil' Dave looked into Jeremiah's eyes at that very moment. It was the first time he'd ever seen him in person, though he'd heard plenty. He right away sensed somethin' that most sense when they look into his eyes—a real captivatin' sincerity.

It's like, whatever you might be feelin' or thinkin' takes second place, and all of a sudden you know Johnson is in control—of a situation and of himself. You then become both curious and eager to listen to what he has to say. You give him the floor so to speak—willingly and without question, even if you don't really know who he is by name.

There's just somethin' about him that permits you to trust in him. It's a rare quality in a man, but it's there. My Granddad (his brother) knew it. My Dad was right there in that cave and told me about it when I was just a boy, and now I'm tellin' you about it. Jeremiah Johnson was a unique man—like no other my Dad ever knew. It would be real nice—a fine thing, if we could all be like him—'more' than trustworthy.

At Jeremiah's request those lawmen put away their guns, and then brought their horses on inside the cave, out of the rain, to mingle with the other horses. They stowed the saddles and blankets on the floor, then the three of 'em moved toward the fire to dry out a little bit as Jeremiah spoke to 'em—spoke to everyone that mornin' around that fire, more or less.

I'm glad my Dad and my two aunts—Carrie and Hannah—were there. They taught me everything they heard that mornin', along with some other things they learned on that trip West. I've been livin' by the things they learned and passed onto me from that experience ever since. It's hard not to want to. There just don't seem to be no other way to live that makes any sense! What Jeremiah said makes *real* sense—and this is what he said to 'em—pay attention, now:

"We've pretty much all made our share of mistakes—more than our share, I reckon. Sometimes it takes awhile before we learn anything from them. I fought with men all my life, but after a while, I came to learn that I was really fighting with myself. My outward battles were more or less a portrayal of my own inward battles—I didn't know that.

"We were born into this world as children of men. Our fathers and forefathers struggled and fought all their lives—and they each died, leaving that legacy to us. We don't change—we can't change. We just keep on living our lives like them, by what we've been taught and with what we feel—that's our nature. It's who we are.

"Sometimes we try different things—ride along with a new idea or two, and some of us go with any wind that blows—but we never really change. Life goes on and we go on with the flow. But, fact is, the only thing that goes with the flow are dead fish. Not even the hungriest critters in the forest will have anything to do with them. It's time we took notice.

"Laws don't change us, or make us any better. When laws are made we look for ways to break them—that's our nature. Think about it. Anyone who says otherwise is a liar—deceiving himself or herself.[1] We have a natural rebellion deep down inside. Laws only provoke it—they don't correct it.

"Men and women have always been our teachers in the things of this life, but there comes a time when that mold we were born into has to be broken. We have to seek something higher than ourselves. That's the only way we can learn who we really are. Bear with me here for a bit...

"I've lived with the rocks and the trees, with the animals and the birds—for years. After a while I began to learn something from them. They've taught me many, many deeper things about life, and I'm still learning. My time alone in the wilderness was a good thing.[2] My relations with the Native Americans has brought that learning along even a bit further. But let me just start with the rocks and the trees."

By this time the lawmen had seated themselves alongside the others at the fire. The rain was still comin' down outside— a mite heavy too. Yet, that was a good thing. The sound of rain and the smell of rain are soothin' to the spirit of a man, or a woman, and that comfort was downright fittin' for the words Jeremiah was speakin' to those folks—words that I myself have come to truly understand and appreciate—especially in the rain.

"There's no two rocks or trees alike, and it's the same with men, or women. We have to take notice of the rocks and the trees—let them teach us about their individuality. I've climbed these high rocks around here many times. You might say I got to know them. Of course, they don't talk back in our language, so knowin' them takes some time. But they're content—they never change—they just keep on bein' rocks and are immovable.

"The wind blows against them, the rain soaks them down and the snow covers 'em, but it doesn't rile them none— they're just content with what they are. After a while, you remember them by their shapes, their cracks and crags—their individual features. You count on them to always be the same. And so, they remain as you've counted on them to remain.

"Now, the trees are a little more fragile. The wind can bend them or break them—tear off their branches and damage their trunks, the snow can droop 'em way down for a spell; yet, they still hang around—unless a mighty big gale comes along and uproots them. They hang around loyal to where they've been placed. You get to know them too.

"Their story is a little different than that of the rocks, but they share a common truth—they know God made them. He made them what they are and he gave them a purpose. The rocks have taught me that God is strong, among other things. The trees have taught me that he is tender. Both have taught me that he is faithful. Though neither of them shares all the same qualities, they've taught me that I can have their combined qualities, because I was made in the image of God.

"Now, about the animals and birds. They're unlike the rocks and trees, on account of being able to move about by their own free will. Free will is a mighty big privilege. The birds can go far greater distances than the animals, and travel much faster. They don't need much to survive, and have the pleasure of seeing things from a vantage point that we can only see if we climb to the top of Mt. Whitney, back up yonder.

"It would take me a three or four day's ridin' to reach that summit, but the hawk? It would be no time at all and he'd be up there—and he could start from farther away than me—miles away. If you watch the birds, you can see that they have certain patterns in their flight. They know where to go when it's hot, and they know where to go when the snow flies—my niece here is learning about all that in her school, back east.

"They can see all kinds of food from the air, and can dive quick. They know where to build their houses, and they protect themselves in ways past findin' out. They've taught me how much wiser God is than all mankind. I'm in awe of their

104

majesty. I can't be like them, so I've learned to be humble instead, because in many ways, they are much greater than me —they have some particular abilities that I—that I just don't have.

"Let's take the animals. I've tracked bear and learned their ways. I've followed the wolves and the coyotes and seen them in their dens. I've watched the beaver build his dam, and I've seen the mountain lion stalk its prey. These animals have taught me how to hunt and how to build—how to live off the land. Again, I'm humbled, and so I've learned to honor them. And I have God's Great Spirit to thank for makin' them my teachers.

"And they oughta' be my teachers! They were created *before* mankind. No man can teach you what the rocks, the trees, the birds, and the animals can—about strength and tenderness, about staying put or bending with the wind, about faithfulness, about loyalty, about watchfulness—they're always alert to what's goin' on around them.

"And I swear—the way the birds and animals protect and care for one another within their families, well, that tells me a love story that's difficult to comprehend. It's a love story that started somewhere before our time—before our time as humans —before them animals and birds—before them rocks and trees, as well.

"Now, through what I've learned, I look around at all humans and I see them differently than I did when I was younger. Most of them don't know anything about the rocks and the trees, nor about the birds and the animals. If they did, they would know a little bit more about who they themselves are. They would come to learn that they are all alike—prone to wander in this life, and prone to mistakes that hurt others and drive a wedge between folks—it's like splittin' a chunk of wood and watchin' the pieces scatter.

"Now, if each man or woman would stop long enough to listen and learn from these things God has made around them, they might find out that faithfulness, loyalty, strength, tenderness, watchfulness, and love and forgiveness toward one another is the path to understanding—the path to peace. It's gotta' start with us. And, as individuals, it don't start with someone else.

"It starts when we each look at ourselves and see what our ignorance of God and our ignorance of all that he's made has done to us. We've got to smother the flames of that rebellion we tote around. We owe it to him to start trusting in his ways and leave selfish interests and traditions behind—we need to look to doin' good to others—to other folks all over this country—white or red or any other color. Color don't separate nobody—it's the attitude of the heart that separates.

"The world can only change by one person at a time making a change for the better of the whole. When we know someone who wants to make that change, we need to get right in there tooth and nail and help them. We owe it to 'em! When a person steps out into the sunlight for the first time, I for one ain't gonna' poke a stick in their eyes so they can't see.

"These three men here told me they were ready to make a change. And I hope that now they might understand what kind of change they really need to make. It's really an attitude change. A man or woman can't change being who they are or what they do, but they sure can change how they go about it, which will eventually, in a spiritual sort of way, change who they are and what they do.

"Now, in the case of these three men, they told me they would give up the money, stop runnin' and robbin', and that they would make a new start by going to work for me at my place. Now, that don't change who they are or what they've done—again, none of us can change who we are. But we can strive toward becoming something better, as I said. And again,

106

all of this knowledge comes to us through nature—through the things God has made."

Johnson looked directly at Lil' Dave and his companions. "You boys can help them with this, if you're of a' mind to."

Harry Brown was the first to speak. "What about what they've done? They've hit three of my banks in the last month, and they surely don't have all that money. I'm sure, Mr. Johnson, that they threw most of it away on immoral women or gambling—or who knows what?"

"No, I don't figure they do have that money," Johnson agreed. "But what about you, Mr. Brown—you ever do something you couldn't undo?"

Harry Brown was silent for a few moments. "I suppose so —we all have—who hasn't?"

"How did you reckon with it, or how do you live with it?"

"—I guess you're right about being guilty of some things. I can't justify them. I've hurt some people. I did what I could to make it up to them—but I guess you can never really do enough to really clear your conscience—unless you just don't care about clearin' it."

"Do you care, Mr. Brown? Do you care enough to forgive these men and accept the loss, in order to better them?"

"The people who bank at Wells Fargo are not going to like that, Mr. Johnson. I know they have the Big Pine money here, and perhaps a portion of the other money as well. Perhaps the residents in Big Pine won't hold a grudge, because they'll get their money back. It's the residents in Sacramento and Auburn and Reno I'm thinking about. They probably won't see ten cents on the dollar! They won't like that!"

"And if they could pay it all back, would everything be okay then?"

"They can't pay it back—they'd be working it off for a hundred or more years."

"Exactly," Jeremiah replied. "But *you* have a choice right now, and the authority within yourself to forgive them. All three of you lawmen do."

"But it's not our money, Mr. Johnson. If it was our money, then that would be a different story altogether."

Jeremiah was silent for a moment—but he soon came back with somethin' you wouldn't expect—not in this lifetime.

"Well, how about I go to trial and serve these men's sentences for them? On top of that, how about I pay back all the money they owe to the banks? —How about I take on these burdens of theirs as my own? The Lord did that for all of us. I might as well do my part—don't you think?"

"Now, wait a minute, Mr. Johnson. You aren't the Lord, and you can't bear these men's burdens for them. That's a— well, that's a religious thing."

"No, Mr. Brown, you're wrong. I was taught that we were to bear one another's burdens. That's what love is all about, which has nothing to do with religion. You can tell those folks in Sacramento and Auburn and Reno that they can go on holding a grudge, but whatever they measure out to these men will be measured out to them, whether they get their money back or not.[3] That's just the way it is. True forgiveness is bigger than all of us—but if we don't practice it, we won't receive it in return.

"Actions speak louder than words. Think about that, Mr. Brown. Go out there among the rocks and trees and sit yourself down. Reach out your hand and touch them—feel their strengths and consider their weaknesses. Talk to the birds and the animals. Learn of their loyalty to their maker—and consider their wisdom. Then, start to think about the way things *should* be among men and not the way they are. Accepting the way things are is for fools—dead fish that go with the flow.

108

"Consider, Mr. Brown, if you will, that things are the way they are because of the way we humans have been—for thousands of years. Think about these children here—about what you'd want to teach them—about how you would want them to act—or react. That's what you need to do, Mr. Brown. You're an educated man—educated by the world's philosophies, but don't let that rule you—you're still just a man."

Lil' Dave spoke up. "He's right, Harry. While listenin' to Johnson I put myself in the place of these men here. A man can get mighty inspired with a fresh start in life, and that's exactly what these men would be getting—and we'd be the ones givin' it to them."

Lil' Dave was a mite excited about the words comin' out of himself—even stood up all of a sudden and began pacin' around to finish his point.

"Now, knowin' I'd be a part of that, well, maybe I could learn to forgive myself for some of the bad things I've done. I'd turn out to be a better person myself! Lord knows I've made my share of mistakes, but, by doin' this for these men, I'm gonna' look at life a mite different—I swear—this is down right motivatin!'—One person at a time, right, Jeremiah?"

"You're a fair man, Lil' Dave—more than fair. What I've heard about you is then true. How about your partner, Marshal Gilmore there?" Johnson turned his eyes on Doc Gilmore, who knew he expected an answer.

"—I can live with it—letting these men go. Made my share of mistakes too. But, I'm not in charge here."

Johnson looked at Harry Brown. "What say you, Harry?"

"I'm not in charge either, Mr. Johnson. Lil' Dave's the law. I'll go along with whatever he recommends."

"What if things were different," Johnson responded. "What if I had suggested that we should hang these men—right outside there on that big oak? Would you boys say you weren't in charge then—that Lil' Dave was the law?"

Harry Brown and Doc Gilmore did not respond. I don't know if they wanted to and couldn't, or just wouldn't? It might be that they just didn't know how to respond. Jeremiah had thrown a lot at 'em. I figure they were plum confounded.

God's teachin's have a way of doin' that—they're meant to —so that men can learn to abandon their foolishness and seek his wisdom, which don't come through our normal way of thinkin'. The world's wisdom is powerful deceptive, and we've all suffered from it.[4] It's been goin' on for thousands of years—pretty hard to unwind somethin' that's been a' coilin' up that long.

Though he didn't get a response, Jeremiah never lost his patience. He figured, though, that he needed to add somethin' to what he had said. When he started out again he spoke right at Doc Gilmore and Harry Brown. But as he went on, he figured he'd look around at everybody there. They all needed to hear it.

Sure, those men were the most doubtful, but he figured it just wasn't his place to let 'em know that he knew that. He was a man who had learned to respect another's feelins'—right or wrong. God is the only one in charge of seein' that men reap what they sew. If Jeremiah couldn't get their attention, he knew that God eventually would—one way or another. He was just tryin' to make it easier on 'em.

"There's one more thing I want you to think about—want you *all* to think about. When God first made man, they didn't need kings or presidents, laws or judges—they just needed to trust in him, and things would work out fine. But, mankind went their own way and broke that trust. They just couldn't see the Creator in what he'd made—wouldn't take the time to think deep enough and to contemplate what was really there.

"So, God allowed that there would be kings and presidents, laws and judges, in order that they would learn to trust. The Good Book says that these things—his law and authorities and ordinances—things that God was more or less forced to allow, were like a schoolmaster—were like a tutor that would lead us to Christ.

"You might say it was like someone escorting children down a long, winding road—protecting them and teaching them along the way. Making sure that the children would actually get to where they set out for in the first place. That destination is pure faith, belief and trust in Jesus Christ, the Son of God, which does away with kings and presidents, with laws and judges—the schoolmasters or tutors.[5]

"God intended for us to love, which, believe it or not, does away with our need for law and punishment. We only have those things because we don't love. Again, God had to institute those things because of our rebellious nature. But love allows for forgiveness, which can smother that fire of rebellion.

"And like I said earlier, it starts with each one of us—starts when we choose to love and forgive our fellow man, or woman. That's what separates us from the world. That's what makes us the children of God—big difference between the children of God and the children of men. All I'm saying is, we need to put that into practice. If we believe in it and work at it, I figure it will work—right up until the Lord comes back and makes everything right."

As Jeremiah finished what he was sayin', his eyes just happened to fall on Marshal Swearengin. When the marshal saw that, he looked around and found the others were lookin' at him as well—everyone in the cave. I guess he felt he was in the spotlight, and I figure he was, since Doc Gilmore and Harry Brown sort of put him there—right smack into it with that, 'we're not in charge' thing. Lil' Dave then spoke up.

"I'm going to think on these things some more. Give me some time, Johnson—just so I know that what I'm doin' is best. We can talk about it some more when we get down the mountain. 'Till then these men are in your custody—under your trust. You'll be responsible, should they decide to run."

Marshal Swearengin then addressed the three men seated at the fire. "I'm not sure why I'm doin' this—it's not a—not a normal thing a US Marshal does. This man believes in you boys. I never heard no town preacher talk like that! His words have spun my mind into circles—for now. And, for some unknown reason, I feel I should go along with him—with his way of thinkin'. I hope you don't let him down. I wouldn't want to break a trust with Jeremiah Johnson, if I were you."

"I know my men," Valencia responded. "I give my word, senor, and I give my word for my compadres here. It's the first time in my life I've ever give my word for anything—and I somehow know I'll keep it." He looked momentarily at San Dona and Chapman. Johnson watched him, and could read sincerity in his eyes—in the eyes of San Dona and Chapman as well.

I believe that was his power. Long ago, Paints-His-Shirt-Red had said that Johnson could read a man's heart. I know that sounds strange. It was most likely God that did the heart readin', then passed it onto Jeremiah—He does work in mysterious ways. But this gift made some of the Crow warriors afraid of him—considered him a spirit of some kind or another.

As he chased down those warriors in the earlier days, some of 'em would begin to chant to the spirits—for protection. The ones that Johnson heard chantin', well, he would let 'em be—let 'em go. He had his own way of thinkin' about the spirits, good or bad, and he never went against his instincts.

Those Crow that were brave enough or stupid enough to come after him, well, he figured they weren't very spiritual, and he was right—every one of 'em lost in their tussle with him and ended up dead. That's the price one pays for pride and ignorance.

"We'll give you back this money, senor—and we got some left over from the Reno bank," Valencia continued. "We'll give you that as well, and we'll stay with Johnson until this thing is ironed out—no runnin'—ain't no where to go anymore. Anyplace you go is like where you been—los resultados son iguales."

"Good enough," Lil' Dave nodded.

Jeremiah looked over at the children. He looked at Shay and the old railroader as well. He didn't want to disappoint nobody, but there had to be a change in his plans. He glanced back at the children. "I think we all ought to go back down to my ranch and get ready for a fine Christmas." He then turned and spoke to Ed and Ron.

"I'm inviting you, these marshals, Harry Brown, and these former outlaws to share Christmas with us. The Perez family will have their brood over there, along with some orphan children as well. When the holiday festivities come to an end, I'll put these men to work at the ranch and guide you boys on over to Mineral King. Might be heavy snow up there right now anyway, with all this rain. We need to change course right now —with the circumstances being what they are. Hope you boys don't mind a slight delay. Sound fair?"

"We may not go to Mineral King, Jeremiah," Ron responded. "I think I've lost that gold fever. I'm in the mood for an old fashioned Christmas myself. It's been a long time since I knowed one. How about you, Ed?"

"Don't know yet. I like driftin'. But, I'm willing to share Christmas with you boys, then wait and see how I feel as the New Year rolls in. Still might need you as a guide after that, Jeremiah, but I ain't in no way disappointed that we're goin' back down now."

"Anytime, Ed—I'll take you over the mountain anytime you want."

Lil' Dave then spoke up. "Jeremiah, I'm going to ride into Lone Pine and get my wife, Georgina, and my boys, Sean and Taylor. I'm sure they would want to meet you and spend the holidays at your ranch, if you don't mind. I think we're going to have a real big celebration, and I want them to be a part of it all."

"I'm honored, Lil' Dave. We best get mounted after breakfast and ride. Hopefully the rain will clear up by then—or turn to snow! You never know for sure what the elements are fixin' to do in the high lonesome. I guess it doesn't really matter, though—whatever they do, there's a reason for it and always a beautiful side to it, in one way or another."

My Dad, though only ten years old at the time, then said somethin' to Windwalker that choked me up a bit when I first heard about it—I guess it still does. It reminded me of how great of a dad he was—and how I miss his great insight:

"Mr. Windwalker, sir, you were right."

"What about, boy?"

"You said that to see a hawk on the wind was a good sign. You were right. The Great Spirit has watched over all of us—especially those three men."

Windwalker then put his arm around the boy. Dad told me years later that he was really honored when the Indian touched him like that—when he showed him that compassion at that particular moment.

He told me to think about what it would be like to know a man who had seen and done so much in his life, and was like a monument among men, and then all of a sudden you feel him put his hand on little ol' you, in kindness—a hand that carried the scars of great battles, yet was gentle on your shoulder and patted at your shoulder like you was really somethin'—like you was his kin!

My Dad never forgot how he felt at that moment. He always said, 'True friendship is when you know that someone really cares about you as a person, and you care about them in the same way.' He said that nuthin' else was more important in this life than that.

He said that friends were like flowers in a field—'they were all a mite different in the way they were arrayed, but come from the same ground, shared the same sun, were blessed by the kiss of the same rain, and were given life by the same God.'

Winter snowstorm approaching Mt. Whitney

Truly His Brother's Keeper
Chapter 8

The rain did indeed turn to snow after breakfast, just as the entire group had left the cave and started down the mountain. It was quite a sight in the High Sierra country—snow clingin' high in the pines and dustin' the rocks along the trail. It was a wet snowfall—uncommon' large, singly diverse flakes that fall feather-light and allow you just a glimpse of their unique designs on the way down.

The riders, passin' through that snowfall, must have felt real good, considerin' what went on in the cave. The array of such fine winter scenery could only add to their serenity and just made it that much better. It was Christmas all around. They would make the ranch a couple days before Christmas Eve, and their attitudes were sure right to make the most of the holiday celebration.

They crossed the trailside meadow about noon and would a short time later begin the arduous climb down Angel's Flight. There was snow on the trail, and that meant a difficult descent along the narrow switchbacks. Jeremiah brought his mount to a halt just above the descent, and then raised a hand toward the other riders, signalin' for them to rein in. He dismounted and peered over the trailhead at the Flight. John Windwalker soon approached on foot, leadin' his mount, and stood beside him.

"What do you think, John?"

"You know how it is, Jeremiah—never looks safe from up here on top, snow or no snow. It is not cold enough for ice, but I think we ought to rope up, just in case."

Johnson and Windwalker had roped up a time or two on this descent. Ropin' up means that the lead rider ties a rope around his waist, and then passes it on back to the next rider, who in turn ties it around his waist and passes it on back to the

117

third rider, with about twenty to thirty feet of slack 'twixt each of the riders. Four to five ropes would have to be used, due to the number of riders on this descent—one rope for each three riders.

Each third rider would have to tie a second rope around his or her waist and pass it on back, so that the whole group would be tied together from the front to the rear of the column. In this way, if one of the horses was to lose it's footin', the combined strength of all the riders would keep that rider from a nasty fall. Could lose a horse, but no one ever heard of that happenin' on the Flight—it was just wise to be prepared for it if it did.

There are a dozen switchbacks on the Flight, each one about fifty or so yards from the other. Goin' up is easy—talked about all this earlier—but comin' back down, that's another story. The trail is steep, strenuous on man or beast, and the shale underfoot can be a mite slippery.

You can't dismount and lead a horse down on foot when you're roped up, 'cause the horse gets in the way of the rope that's 'twixt each of those dismounted. Besides, a man leadin' a horse down a steep incline is trouble for sure. You have to ride—the horse is more sure-footed that way anyhow. Yep—ropin' up and ridin' is the best way to make the descent.[1]

"John, lets put one of the younger folks in the middle of each group in the first three groups. Be safer that way. I think we'll be okay. I'll explain what we're doing and why to all the riders. I don't suppose they've ever done anything like this."

It took about a half hour to get everyone tied together and ready. Everybody ate some snacks, drank some water, and then the descent began. Jeremiah, my Dad, and Railroad Ron took the lead. Behind them were Ed Shay, Hannah, and John Windwalker.

The third group was Lil' Dave, Carrie, and Armando Valencia. Taking up the rear was White Eyes Chapman, Riccardo San Dona, Doc Gilmore, and Harry Brown on the tail. The snow was fallin' heavy, but that was a good thing. When it wasn't cold enough to freeze, that little pad of snow between the shale-strewn trail and the horse's hooves meant surer footin'.

When Jeremiah turned the first switchback he was able to view the entire group above and behind him—all looked good. Thank God there was no wind that afternoon. He checked the train with each turn, riders and their mounts, like an old papa coyote watchin' all his young'uns. He'd speak to the other riders now and again—I 'spose to keep their courage from a' falterin':

"Hey Marc, is your hair standing up, or did your hat shrink?" And, "Hannah, if your face gets any whiter, we won't be able to see you in the snow." He ragged on Ed Shay too. "You sweatin', ol' timer, or did you wet your pants?" Railroad Ron got one thrown at him as well. "If your neck gets any stiffer, we'll have to lay you on your back to pull your boots off." When he cleared the final switchback he asked everyone, "Anyone need to change their underwear?"

Railroad Ron came off the Flight right behind him and my Dad. He looked at my Dad with a big grin and nudged him on the shoulder at the same time.

"History was made today, boy. We rode up Angel's Flight and come back down in one piece—stiff-necked, straight-haired and all—and we rode all that way with Jeremiah Johnson—in the high and mighty Sierra. Now, that's somethin' to tell your grandkids! Who would ever figger that we'd be that fortunate?"

"And we helped some outlaws go straight," my Dad smiled.

That ol' railroader took off his hat and brushed the snow from it. "Let's hope so, boy—let's hope so."

The group soon headed down the boulder-strewn trail descendin' from the Flight, then rode on into the timberline and crossed Horseshoe Meadow. There wasn't any snowfall at that lower elevation and even the sun had come out in all of its radiance. When they got to the far side of the meadow, Jeremiah, still in the lead, brought his mount to a halt at the north fork of Lone Pine Creek. He dismounted as the others caught up and reined in near him.

"Creek's deep here, and a mite cold this time of year, but we've got three baptisms to take care of," he said, speaking to all the riders. "Baptism is a necessity when one turns their life over to God, and it seals their union with the Lord. A person is actually baptized into his death—lowered into a watery grave as it were, and then rises up out of that water to begin a new life.

"A person's old self is dead and buried, so to speak, with Christ, and rises to walk with him in this new life—least ways that's my understanding of the Scriptures.[2] It's kind of a physical thing that ends up being a spiritual thing—that's God's way of looking at it. Some folks say you don't need it, but I've never been one to tell God how to do things. You three men ready for this?"

Valencia, San Dona and Chapman each responded promptly with a "Yes, Sir," to that question.

Jeremiah just smiled as them men clumb down off their horses, and him and Windwalker then led them down the bank and on out into the water. When they got to where it was deep enough they immersed them. Jeremiah told 'em that they were being baptized 'in the name of the Father, the Son, and the Holy Ghost.'

The three of them men were smilin' when they come up out of the water. Everyone standing on the bank give a grin, clapped their hands and nodded their approval. My Aunt Carrie raised her arms toward the sky and shouted, "Halleluiah!" It was a fine thing she done—an even finer thing them three men done!

Ed Shay passed out blankets so that everyone that got wet could mop most all of that water from their clothing. There wasn't any wind, and the sun bein' out in its full splendor helped a little bit. When all was said and done everyone shook the hands of those men, and in a short time all were mounted up and ready to ride on.

They trailed the creek once again and rode through the stands of pines, then descended along the lower ridge until they reached the fork of the Big Pine, Lone Pine, and High Sierra Trails. It was at that junction where Lil' Dave Swearengin split off from the rest of 'em and headed for Lone Pine.

"These men are in your care, Johnson, until I get back over your way tomorrow. Doc and Harry Brown will ride on with you to your ranch and stay there. We'll talk about these ol' boys some more then—figure out just what should be done. I want you to know that I've been thinkin' about what you said —all the way down the mountain."

"Fair enough," Jeremiah answered. "See you tomorrow."

When they got to the ranch they could see a trail of smoke risin' up from the chimney. As they drew nigh on to the cabin the front door opened and David Perez stepped out onto the porch.

"We saw some riders up on the Flight, yonder—figured it was you. The wife's got some stew going. She's down at the house with all them young'uns. I'm just up here watching the pot. Glad you're here—the smell of that fine stew's got me 'bout starved near to death."

"I didn't bring back any elk, Dave," Jeremiah said. "Maybe we can go hunt one over the holidays?"

"No problem, Senor Jeremiah. We'll be cookin' up some ham for the holiday dinner anyway. Got plenty of that. Won't need no meat for a spell. —Looks like you got some company there, Senor Jeremiah?" David Perez was speakin' of the additional three riders.

121

"Found these boys up on the mountain. Old friends—they'll be staying around awhile."

"We'll have a *big* Christmas then, senor," Mr. Perez smiled. "We got a bunch of kids visiting, and the Indian boys are coming up from the orphanage."

"That's good," Jeremiah nodded. "We're going to unpack here and corral the horses—tend to them a bit. A few of us will need some dry clothing, too—if you could bring out a few pairs of pants and shirts and underwear from that cedar chest beside my bunk? I'd appreciate it. Bring the clothing on out to the barn, if you would. —Stew sounds mighty good—we'll be in directly—before it's all gone," he laughed.

Sometime later, after a real fine dinner, Jeremiah invited Windwalker, Ed Shay, Railroad Ron, Armando Valencia, Riccardo San Dona, White Eyes Chapman, Doc Gilmore and Harry Brown out onto the front porch to set a spell. He'd been thinkin' about some things all the way down the mountain, and wanted to talk to everyone concerned. My Dad and my two aunts come outside and wanted to join the group as well.

"Fine," said Jeremiah. "Grab a seat and listen up—it'll be good that you hear all this."

"I want you boys—and girls—all to know what I plan on doing, and I'd like to hear how you all feel about it. It's Christmas—almost anyway, and I'm feeling its mood. I been blessed—all my life actually, and I feel that I have a duty to do something about that. It took me a lot of years to actually see the blessings through all the hardships, but I'm truly thankful for them now—kinda' changes one's perspective.

"I got nearly 5000 acres here—all good land—lots of pine and lots of good growin' land also, if one is a' mind to planting. Got some stock, but there's a lot of free roaming cattle and horses over Nevada way that could be brought here and sold to the army. There's other buyers up north as well—

122

even down south, and they're always looking for good stock at a fair price.

"Now, I know that the Deputy Marshal here and Harry Brown have their own lives and there own business to attend to, but the rest of you boys can work for me and we'll build this ranch into a good business. We'll build a bunkhouse and some more corrals. The barn I got now is plenty big enough.

"Now, if you boys work at this, and we get things set up by summer's end, then I'll give you each 300 acres of my land as your own. We'll divide another thousand acres into four plots, build cabins on each one, and sell the lots to folks who want to settle in this area. We'll take the money from those sales and pay back the banks that you former outlaw boys stole from. Anything left over gets divided among the five of you.

"John and me will have plenty with the 2500 acres that are left. All the ranch stock will be kept on that part of the land, along with any we bring in from elsewhere. Whatever we do bring in, you boys can keep the best pick of the horses we round up on each run, at your own place—you don't have to mix them in with the animals that belong to the business.

"You'll each get a stud and a mare in your pick, that way you'll have a chance to build your own herds and do with them as you see fit. Raising horses and a few other animals on the place—even dogs, is a fine thing—keeps a man's thoughts on the simpler things in life. Any cattle we round up will of course be strictly for the business—US Army's always needin' beef. No call for us to be hording them.

"Now, that's my Christmas present to each of you. Armando—you, San Dona and Chapman will have to stay on until the four smaller parcels I talked about are built up and sold off. After that you can stay here on your own parcel and work for me as long as you want—roundin' up and sellin' stock. But your land will be your land. Any of the mustangs that we're partial to and don't want to sell, we'll divide up amongst all of us—I ain't greedy.

"We can take some time off whenever you feel like it—go into the mountains, go fishing or hunting—whatever. Them's my words in this matter. Speak up if have a problem with 'em.

"Ed and Ron, you have no obligation to any of this. You boys are free as the wind, and you can stay on as long as you like. Your portion of the land and stock will remain yours, stay or go. But, Armando, Riccardo and White Eyes will have to work off the debt to the banks—through buildin' up and selling those small parcels I mentioned—I think I said that earlier, didn't I?

"But, it's not actually going to be a debt to the Wells Fargo company—per se. I'm going to pay back what you owe up front. That will make Harry Brown here a happy man. You boys will then owe me. So, if you don't stick it out, at least you'll be free in respect to the folks whose money was in those banks.

"A man should pay back what he owes, but I won't come after you to collect for myself. I just figure you'll chose to do what's right—I think you've done that already, and I figure you'll hold to it. You'll all be paid for your work as well. A man who rides for the brand should draw its wages—unless he's out there somewhere on the range, asleep on his watch.

"I am well aware, though, that sometimes we don't always do what we should. That's why I won't hold it against you if you saddle up and ride out early. Things change from day to day. We each have our own problems, our own pressures, and our own ways of dealing with them.

"I'm easy to work with—easy to get along with. I'll treat you boys fair and take an interest in you personally. Your problems will be mine—and we'll work through them, in hopes that you'll stick it out. That's just the way it is—that's the way I am—up front and no frills."

Jeremiah leaned back and lit a pipe. He didn't do that often, but when he did, you knew he was satisfied with the way things were goin' in his life. He told my Dad that the smoke took up his prayers to God—somethin' he learned from the Crow. Just after he packed and lit that pipe, Valencia, San Dona and Chapman took their turns at talkin' to him. They said that what he offered them was more than they'd ever known—said it was like steppin' out of reality and walkin' into a dream.

They said it was a right beautiful place to work, too—that just watchin' the sunset at the ranch was mighty encouragin', and that a man could work all day and put everything he had into that work, knowin' that he had such a spectacle to look forward to, come evenin'. Sunrises in the Sierra are indeed spectacular as well, and the mornin' air gives a body strength and carries him the whole day—makes him appreciate the God who formed each of these created things—things that most of us just take for granted.

Doc Gilmore and Harry Brown were in awe at Jeremiah's generosity. They said that it was a mighty kind thing he was a' doin' for the hopes and dreams of those men. They said it was the kind of thing that all of us were lookin' for, but dang few of us ever get to see it.

Johnson told them that sometimes you got to put your faith it what you can't see. He told them that love was the answer to all of the world's problems, and that the whole of it all was that love was summed up in kindness and doin' things for and with others. He said if folks would consider each man or woman as an equal, and strive to have all things in common, then it would be only natural for one to share or sell his possessions and goods and divide them among others, as anyone had need.

He summed it all up by sayin' that life was all about sharin', and about enjoyin' and appreciatin' everything that God had made. He said there was no call for a man to worship his own possessions. A man's blessed in what he owns and gives, not in what he keeps and takes.[3]

The visitors all camped out in the main room of the cabin that night and were up before first light. There were a few chores that needed to be done, and so after breakfast everyone pitched in. About noontime Lil' Dave Swearengin rode in with his wife and two sons. His wife continued on over to the Perez place with the boys, as all the younger folks were over there and involved in gettin' things ready for the holidays.

Sean and Taylor Swearengin were in their late teens, and the eldest of all the younger folks. They were good boys— raised fine and proper, and helped with the supervision of all the other youngsters in their activities at the Perez place. It was the first time Georgina Swearengin ever met Sheri Perez, and they hit it off real good. There was a lot to do, and everyone was havin' a great time doin' it.

At the Johnson ranch, Lil' Dave was informed of Jeremiah's plans for the three former outlaws. Jeremiah had taken him out on the porch, where they could talk alone. Lil' Dave said that he had thought about things all the way down the mountain the day before, and had then spoke to his wife about them when he rode back to Lone Pine.

Lil' Dave told Jeremiah that he always talked things over with his wife. Said he felt right good about it because the Lord meant for things to be that way between a man and a woman. He said that the two of them decided that forgivin' those men was a fine thing that Jeremiah had proposed, and that he would do everything he could to see that no one would know who those robbers were, and that they could straighten out their lives at the Johnson ranch without anyone ever knowin' anything about their past. He would just tell folks that the real bank robbers had just disappeared—that he'd lost their trail. In a way, he'd be tellin' 'em right.

126

Said he figured he wouldn't be lyin'. He said as far as he was concerned, their outlaw ways *had* disappeared—they was no longer set on bein' the kind of men that they had been. There weren't no posters or pictures of 'em that he knew of, and after all, who wouldn't doubt that any outlaw could work for Jeremiah Johnson? Everyone in that part of the country felt that he was always partial to upstandin' folk. His character was one that nobody in the High Sierra country would dispute.

Shortly after that conversation, Lil' Dave got the money together that needed to be returned to the bank in Big Pine, and rode off to town with his deputy and Harry Brown to do just that. Jeremiah told Harry to let him know how much was owed to the Wells Fargo Company in Sacramento, Auburn and Reno. Harry told him he would do that sometime after the holidays He said he was goin' back to Reno to spend Christmas with his family.

When the lawmen were about a quarter mile down the road, Lil' Dave turned his horse around all of a sudden, told the other lawmen to wait where they was, and rode at a gallop back to the front porch of the cabin, where Jeremiah was still standin'. When he brought his mount to a halt he just sat there for a time in thought—then he scratched at his head a bit and looked up at Jeremiah on the porch.

"You know, Jeremiah, that I'm gonna' have to make up a story about how we got all those folks money back. I got to thinkin' that it might be a bit hard to explain. I want this whole thing to come out right. Any ideas on how we go about explainin' the money situation to folks—I mean, how do you get all the money without catchin' the men? Losin' their trail but still bringin' back the money seems a mite strange, don't it?"

"How about this, Lil' Dave—tell them you found the money on the bank of Rush Creek, where the trail disappeared. Tell them you found a note with it. Tell them the note said,

'Merry Christmas to all the folks of Big Pine.' No one can explain things that happen at Christmas, and no one is going to expect you to explain such a thing. If they do, you just tell 'em them old boys must've had a change of heart—after all, it is Christmas."

Lil' Dave smiled like you never seen. He liked the idea fine. He told Jeremiah also that he would talk to Sheriff Ken Petty about this whole matter of the outlaws, and was confident that ol' Petty would keep things under his hat for the sake of his friend, and that the sheriff would treat those men with respect from that point on, and would never let on to folks that he knew anything about them—anything about their past livin'.

About the same time Lil' Dave rejoined the other lawmen and rode off to Big Pine, Sheri Perez, Georgina Swearengin and my aunt Carrie hitched a wagon and headed out for the orphanage in Lone Pine to pick up the three Indian boys. They returned with them before sundown. Lil' Dave and Doc Gilmore rode back to the ranch that night, and would stay on for the festivities the next day, which was Christmas Eve.

On Christmas Eve mornin', after everyone ate pancakes, sausage and bacon at the Johnson ranch, Ed Shay and Railroad Ron rode off to town—said they had to do some shoppin'. John Windwalker decided at the last minute to go with 'em. He said it was a fine day and he wanted to tag along for the ride, and, well, my Dad was right there to ride along with him. Him and Windwalker grew pretty close that Christmas.

I should tell you before I go on with this story that my Dad and Windwalker wrote letters back and forth for years after that special Christmas. Jeremiah wrote a couple himself. But one day, my Dad got a letter from Windwalker—early in 1928— that said that Jeremiah had passed on late in 1927, and that Windwalker had laid him up in the Sierras that year near a place called Mirror Lake. My Dad passed on many years ago, in 1963, but when I went through his things I never found that particular letter.

One letter said that Ed Shay had rode off for Yosemite after Jeremiah died, and was never heard from again. Another said that Railroad Ron had gone to Montana to work on the biggest horse ranch in the territory, owned by a former Captain of the Texas Rangers—a man named Woodrow F. Call. That letter went on to say that he was hired on as the ranch foreman—somethin' about nobody else up there havin' enough sand to handle the job?

Still another letter, an earlier one, said that Valencia, San Dona, and Chapman were still at the ranch, had paid all their debts, and were buildin' new homes for a passel of arrivin' settlers. They had a reputation in town as fair and honest men —now ain't that somethin'?

That letter was dated 1918—about nine years before Jeremiah had died. He helped those men, and lived to see the fruit of both his labors and theirs. I was real happy when I read that letter. I'm sure my dad was too, at the time.

I sure would like to have been there at the time—to share that happiness with him. I wasn't even born yet. My ma did, though—she shared it with him—later on. I know I ain't said much about my ma in this story. Her name was Pauline Johnson. She passed on a few years before dad. She got the cancer at a fairly young age—thirty-eight, she was. I was only 'bout fourteen when she passed, and she had just turned forty-one—that was 1959.

She was much younger than dad. He was born in 1880, and ma was born in 1918. They married in 1940, and loved each other for the rest of their lives. She really didn't have much to do with this story, other than the fact that if that precious thing hadn't of married my dad, I wouldn't be here to tell the story. But she was real close to dad, and they shared everything.

129

I know that, because both of them told me parts of this story—many times—and ma wasn't even there! My dad was only ten at the time—when all this happened, and ma wasn't even born yet. But, I grew up hearin' it from both sides. So, I know that her and dad must have talked about this story to one another all the time. I'm glad they did. What they passed onto me shaped my life. Now, I'm passin' it on to you. I hope you can glean from it as well.

The last letter my Dad got from Windwalker was in the winter of 1929. He said he was bound for Colorado. He said that Valencia and Chapman had passed on from this life, and were buried down in the Lone Pine cemetery.

Valencia was real sick the previous winter, and one day just rode off—rode up the mountain toward Mirror Lake. Windwalker found him about a week later, sittin' against a pine tree—the man was froze to it. He said his eyes were open, though, and there was a smile on his face.

Chapman died just about a year later in the bunkhouse. He got some kind of infection. I guess his old, tired body just couldn't fight it off. Doc Gilmore was there and he was a' cryin'. —Ol' Doc had give up drinkin' and carousin' and went back to practicin' medicine, but there was nuthin' he could do for the man—no cure for his ills.

Riccardo San Dona had been sittin' in the room with Chapman each night, after his fever come on. The letter said John Windwalker was in the room there as well at the last. He said that Chapman's partin' words were mighty encouragin':

"I'm so light headed…I can hardly…can hardly talk or think, but I heard a fella once say, that if God is with a man when he dies, he'll see a white light a' shinin' round about him —ever so bright!"

"John," he said, lookin' straight into Windwalker's eyes, "I see that white light." He then closed his eyes and, well, just went to sleep, John wrote. He was gone—he was just gone.

John said him and San Dona broke down and cried with Doc Gilmore for a time. They was all busted up over it.

The letter said that San Dona lit out for Reno not long after that—somethin' about him workin' in communications. That ol' boy married some gal up there and become an instructor in his line of work, whatever it was—Windwalker didn't know too much about them new fangled things that ol' San Dona was into. He said he was runnin' for an office of some kind as well —State Senator, or somethin' like that.

Windwalker then sold the ranch a few months later 'cause everyone was gone. He sold it to some packin' outfit, the letter said—some fellers that offered guided horse trips into the Sierras. I think their grandchildren are still runnin' the place. I often wonder if they know its history? The parcels belongin' to them other cowboys had been sold to newcomers—all except Ed Shay's parcel. Windwalker figured Ed might come back some day, from wherever he was, and would be a' wonderin' what happened to his land.

But, like I said, the letter about Jeremiah's death, which was probably written in early '28, I never found among my Dad's things. I swear—I searched everywhere for that letter. I know my Dad wouldn't have told me about Jeremiah dyin' and not kept the letter. Never found it. But, somethin' happened last week that was *mighty* strange—mighty strange indeed.

What happened last week is the reason I'm tellin' you this whole story. I told you at the very beginning that I had my reasons for tellin' it. Well, I'm gonna' tell you just what did happen last week—and you'd best be sittin' down when I do, but I need to finish the story first. That way, you might be able to make *some* sense out of what I'm gonna' say to you about what happened last week—you'll just have to trust me and hear me out. The rest of the story has to come first. As Jeremiah would have said, 'that's just the way it is.'

Wolf Tail Lake on the Johnson Ranch

A High Sierra Christmas
Chapter 9

On Christmas Eve, everyone had gathered at the ranch. It had been snowin' since noon and it was both a beautiful and fittin' sight to behold. The cabin was full of folks. There were no single gatherin's of any particular age group of folks, nor were they grouped together by things they might have in common, but instead, every one of all ages and various interests were minglin' together. I 'spect it was a fine thing to be a part of.

Jeremiah and Valencia were playin' cards with Hannah in front of the fireplace. Jeremiah got up now and then to throw a new log on the fire. White Eyes Chapman was tellin' stories to the three orphan boys nearby. Riley Virginia, Mikey and Joseph Perez had gathered around to listen to those tales as well. I'm sure they got an ear full. White Eyes was full of wind, but Windwalker said that as the years rolled on by, it turned into a mighty good wind.

San Dona and Windwalker were shootin' marbles with Carrie and my Dad. Sheri Perez and Georgina Swearengin were addin' more decorations around the room and onto the Christmas tree, and Bryce and Cael Perez were helpin' them. Bryce's dog, old Sam, was there as well, but spent most of his time curled up in front of the fireplace—raisin' his head and perkin' up his ears every now and then as he watched the goin's on. He behaved well, for bein' part wolf and all.

The lawmen, Lil' Dave and Doc Gilmore, were makin' popcorn balls for the tree. They'd tease the younger children once in a while, threatenin' to wipe their sticky hands on 'em. Railroad Ron was roamin' around, minglin' with all the different groups and offerin' his humor—in one way or another. He was one to poke fun at some things now and again, but in a kind way. Windwalker said he was about the most easy goin' fella he'd ever knowed.

Ed Shay was at work in the kitchen with David Perez and the Swearengin boys, Sean and Taylor. A couple of great big hams was on the spit, and that group was puttin' together a menu of green beans, scalloped potatoes, salad, cornbread, and a variety of Christmas pies and other treats, includin' wild apple cider and fresh lemonade. Makes me come into a powerful hunger just thinkin' about it all.

Sheriff Ken Petty rode up just about suppertime. Ol' Petty liked to talk about his fishin' trips—'specially about the bigger fish that got away. Ed Shay would always tease him about the way he measured them fish—said they got bigger each time he told the story. Lil' Dave said he was always a fine companion to have around at suppertime—he kept everyone laughin' and always pitched in at doin' dishes and cleanin' up.

Sheriff Petty was one to listen when others talked as well, and always offered some interestin' philosophy along the way. Lil' Dave said things were never borin' when he was around. Said his stories stretched things every which way, and kept one's mind occupied, separatin' the fact from the fiction—but they was all good stories.

Windwalker said Ed Shay later took to fishin' with the sheriff most all the time—got to tellin' a few stories himself. Somehow, everything ol' Shay pulled in was always a mite bigger than what the sheriff caught. He said ol' Petty always scowled at Shay when he talked like that.

At the dinner table (they had pushed three long tables together, near the fireplace) Jeremiah laid out his plans to all the folks for the three men, Armando Valencia, White Eyes Chapman, and Riccardo San Dona. Everyone was real happy about it all and said that it made for a fine Christmas story. The two adult women started cryin', and then got up from their seats, made their way over to where the three men were seated, and commenced to hug them. Got a couple of them men cryin' as well.

After dinner everybody pitched in at clearin' up the tables and bringin' out the Christmas presents for everyone to open. The warm cider and lemonade was passed around and the festivities began with a prayer. It was John Windwalker who was asked to give those blessin's, as Jeremiah had given the dinner blessin'. Windwalker got up from his seat and knelt down on the floor. Most everyone bowed their heads and some knelt down with him—my Dad was one of 'em.

"Oh, Grand Father, we have been allowed a great thing this day. Your Spirit has walked among us. The wind and the snow have caressed our home. The animals in the forest, in the field, and among the rocks and the trees surround the cabin on this wintry night, and gaze in wonder at your presence. We ask that you walk with us each day, and we ask that you continue to bless us as we celebrate this season of honor.

"I am proud to have been a warrior. Thank you for my victories, and thank you for my defeats, through which I have come to understand greater victories. Thank you for all these people who have become my friends. May we now honor you, through honoring one another with the gifts that you have provided."

After that prayer Jeremiah opened his Bible and read the story of the birth of Christ.[1] He said that the gifts offered to the young Jesus by the wise men were given to honor him as the Son of the Most High God. He said that this became a custom durin' the Christmas season, and so we honor Christ through our gifts to one another. He also said that this spirit of givin' to one another in this manner should be a part of us year 'round.

Followin' the readin' and the truly wise counsel by Jeremiah, Sheri Perez waded through the presents and passed them out, accordin' to the names that had been written on their individual wrappin's. Every one got at least four, but them orphan boys hit the jackpot that Christmas, with about eight or more gifts each. The presents were opened one at a time, so that all could share in the excitement of one another. It was a good custom—somethin' that the Perez family had always done.

The large group had formed a circle for this activity, and when it was one's turn to open a present, he or she had to sit in the middle of that circle. Everyone whooped and hollered as each gift was bein' unwrapped. They offered a variety of comments on the gift, some of which were a mite humorous. Sometimes, though, humans can say the wrong things at a time like this—things that tend to poke fun at the gift or the person receivin' it.

My Dad taught me that this was the worst time to make fun of someone, or his or her gift. He said it was not very encouragin' to either person; giver or receiver—said it was really a meanness that we all have within us—one that we fail to recognize. He said that there were lots of things that cause this attitude—like jealousy or inferiority, or even down right orneriness, but that it was mostly a lack of understandin' and respect for another person's feelin's.

'Words are mighty important,' he told me. He said the tongue is the worst part of our body.[2] He said a small spark can start a great fire. He said it was mighty hard to watch one's words, but that it was the most important thing we could ever think about, and that we should always think before we say or do anything. He was right. I think that's the best advice he ever gave me. I've thought about it all my life—and tried real hard to use it—to live by it.

Some of the presents opened that year at the Johnson ranch were hand made. Ed Shay gave out polished rocks—a hobby he had developed from rock huntin' in the Mojave. Windwalker made some fine bracelets out of beads and turquoise. The blue stone is sacred to the Crow. Railroad Ron gave everyone a railroad spike—don't that beat all? He said one day he figured all the railroads would be turned to rust or gone. I guess a lot of 'em have turned to rust, but there's still trains a'bout—a lot of long haulers on some of the old routes, and they still pass through the high country.

The Swearengin family gave out homemade Christmas cookies. Carrie and Hannah gave out peppermint candy sticks from the general store in Big Pine. Mrs. Perez gave out hand knit gloves, with winter comin' and all. And Jeremiah, well, he liked to make candles. Gave 'em away every year. He mixed sap from the redwood cedars in the wax, and they gave out a fine scent. He said there was nothin' like a smell of the outdoors when you had to be indoors.

I can't remember much about any of the other gifts. My Dad told me these things a long time ago now, and, well, my memory ain't what it use to be. It was a simple Christmas, but a more magnificent one, since the birth of Christ himself, I've personally never heard tell about.

Sheri Perez was the last one to open a present that night. She had arranged things that way because she had somethin' mighty powerful to say to all the folks:

"You all now know the three young Indian boys who are with us tonight. If you don't know their full names, I will ask them to stand up as I recite them. First of all we have Ryan Running Horse—stand up, Ryan. He's fourteen years old, and has been at the orphanage since he was two.

"His parents died in an earthquake many years ago. Ryan is a fine boy, and reads books to the other children at the orphanage. The director of the orphanage, who said that Ryan would go out into the field behind the barn and run a'bout with the horses in the morning, was the person who named him.

"The second young man is Cameron White Eagle." Sheri smiled as the young boy stood up without her promptin' him to do so. He had a big smile on his face.

137

"Cameron is nine years old, and has been at the orphanage from birth. He was found on the steps of the orphanage nine years ago. He rooms with Ryan, and Ryan has taken him under his wing. Cameron likes to garden, and he's planted a little garden at the orphanage, and grows strawberries and tomatoes for his friends there.

"Cameron's name was given him by the school nurse. She said that he would tell her about dreams that he had, in which a large, white eagle would circle over his head as he walked through the rocks above Lone Pine Lake. She said that it was a sign that he would one day be the guardian of a great man.

"The third young man visiting with us is Mason Kicking Bird. He is eight years old. His mother died when he was five, and a friend of the family brought him to the orphanage. His mother had named him 'Kicking Bird,' because he would watch the roosters fight in a neighbor's yard, and would describe them as 'birds that kick.'"

Mrs. Perez tugged on the boys' coat, at which time he stood up next to his two friends. He was a mite shy. "He is very creative at the school. His artwork is the most popular. He draws the mountains—Mt. Whitney and the Needles, and Lone Pine Peak. We are hoping that in time his artwork will become popular among the tourists who visit Lone Pine to hike the high trails. We've been getting quite a few visitors since that man, John Muir, made the climb and lived to tell about it."

When Sheri Perez finished those introductions, everyone in the room suddenly clapped and cheered—some stood up. Mrs. Perez soon raised a hand to quiet everyone down. There was a bit more she wanted to say.

"I want everyone to know that David and I have petitioned for adoption of these boys. The procedure should be final sometime after the New Year. They will come and live with us, and work on projects at the orphanage school two days a week.

They will also continue their education at the Big Pine School with our children as well. We're so happy!"

This time everyone stood up—clappin' and cheerin' once again. What a Christmas, huh? My Dad told me that was the best Christmas he ever had in his life. Aunt Carrie and aunt Hannah said they didn't recollect another one like it neither. At the end of all those festivities, aunt Carrie led every one in fine song of the season. She use to say that she could always hear the voices of everyone there that Christmas—hear' em in her heart—even as the many years rolled by, and right up until she passed on from this life.

On that Christmas Eve she got everybody close together and near that cracklin' fire, askin' them to hold hands, and then she said to everyone, "When Jesus was born, there were shepherds living out in the fields nearby, keeping watch over their flocks at night." Then she started singin' and right away everyone there started singin' with her:

"Silent night, Holy night,
All is calm, All is bright.
Round yon virgin mother and child.
Holy Infant so tender and mild,
Sleep in heavenly peace, Sleep in heavenly peace.

"Silent night, Holy night,
Shepherds quake at the sight.
Glories stream from heaven afar;
Heavenly hosts sing al-lelu-ia.
Christ the Savior is born! Christ the Savior is born!

"Silent night, Holy night,
Wondrous star, lend thy light.
With the angels let us sing,
Al-lelu-ia to our King.

139

Christ the Savior is born! Christ the Savior is born!

"Silent night, holy night,
Son of God, love's pure light.
Radiant beams from Thy holy face,
With the dawn of redeeming grace,
Jesus, Lord, at Thy birth, Jesus, Lord, at Thy birth."

After the song, the young Indian boy, Mason Kicking Bird, smiled at all the folks as he let out with some fine words:
"And God bless us—everyone."

Well—that's near 'bout all I know about that special Christmas celebration, which was shortly before the turn of that century. It's been a long time ago now. As far as I know, everyone in the story is gone—passed on from this life. My family—the Johnson family—is all gone too. Like I said, Dad passed on in '63. Hannah and I buried aunt Carrie in '75.

They're in Lone Pine—and so are most of the folks that shared that Christmas. It's the closest cemetery to the old ranch, and that's where my Dad wanted to be as well. Aunt Carrie was no different. They wanted to be there, and they wanted to leave somethin' there.

Dad's marker reads, 'The Hawk Soars.' Now, ain't that somethin'? He learned a lot about the hawks from Windwalker. It was always his favorite critter. Taught me a lot about their ways too. A hawk always builds its nestin' place high above the ground—on rocky cliffs, or in the trees. They soar high in the air, hover, and can even hold real still up there in a mighty wind. Hawks have powerful wings—span near to five feet— and keen eyesight, too. Their eyesight is near eight times that of a human.

Windwalker told Dad that they were a wise bird, and knew the future. Said they were associated with what was good in

140

that respect, and seein' one in flight was then a sign of good things to come. Dad always said, if he could be anything in another life, or even in this one, he said he would want to be a hawk. And so that's why we did his marker as such.

When aunt Carrie passed on, my aunt Hannah insisted that we carve 'Silent night, Holy night, All is calm, All is bright,' on her stone, and so we did that. That Christmas at the Johnson ranch was always a first in aunt Carrie's heart. She sung that song year round, and at all Christmas's every year after that, and her voice never failed—even in her old age. Taught all her students to sing it, too. I—I can even hear her singin' it as well at that High Sierra Christmas, and I wasn't even there!

Aunt Hannah passed on in 1980. Like I said, she's in Lone Pine too. She was an actress, aunt Hannah. She was in plays all over this country, month after month, year after year. Nobody ever knew she was Jeremiah Johnson's niece, though—kept that to herself. Said she just didn't want to answer no questions about Jeremiah. Said her memories of him were fine the way they were. Her stone reads, 'Sierra Wildflower.' That's what she said she wanted to be, and so she is! They grow plentiful— all around her restin' place.

Well, I am the last of the Johnson's. I figured I was the only one left to tell this story, and I'm the only one who really knows most all about it—only one livin', anyway. Least ways, that's what I've thought for a long time…

141

Crossing Lone Pine Creek in the High Sierra

Epilogue

I told you that I was gonna' tell you about somethin' that happened last week, which was mighty strange—but maybe not so strange after all. I told you, first of all, that I never found the letter that Windwalker wrote to my Dad in 1928—the letter about Jeremiah Johnson's passin' on. Looked high and low, as I also told you, yet never found it.

The letter had said that Jeremiah died in 1927, and was laid to rest at Mirror Lake, which is up a' ways along the Mt. Whitney Trail. The letter also said that no one was to know exactly where Jeremiah was laid—looters and such might get wind of it. Also, the Indians in Utah and Colorado would want to travel out there, just to put bones and handmade trinkets and such all over the spot. Jeremiah was a private man and wanted a private restin' place.

Well, about a week ago now, I got a phone call from a man who said he was the grandson of Cameron White Eagle. If you remember, White Eagle was one of the orphan boys adopted by the Perez family. The grandson said he had somethin' real important to show me, and wanted me to come to Tucson, Arizona, where he now lives.

His name is John Perez—Running Horse is his Indian name. He said he had a letter that John Windwalker had given his grandfather in 1930. It seems that my Dad mailed that letter back to Windwalker, because he didn't want its contents to be found by some eastern newspaperman, who had wind of a story that Jeremiah was wanderin' up in the High Sierras, and had died up there.

When Windwalker got the letter back, he become curious about that twist of fate, and studied its contents, influenced to do so by a vision of some sort. Windwalker then left Colorado to seek out Cameron White Eagle, who was about 50 years old by that time. It was because of somethin' that Mrs. Perez had said about the boy some 40 years earlier.

If you recall, as a youth, Cameron would dream about hikin' up to Lone Pine Lake, in the rocks just above it, and claimed to see a big white eagle flyin' overhead—several different times. The school nurse had afterward named the boy 'White Eagle,' and foretold that he would be the guardian of a great man—remember that?

Windwalker had come to believe that what the boy saw in his dreams was a sign—a sign that Cameron White Eagle was to become, not the guardian of Johnson himself, but the 'keeper of the Johnson legend.'

Lone Pine Lake is just below Mirror Lake on the Whitney Trail. Windwalker did find Cameron, in 1930, in the town of Lone Pine. He told him that his dreams about the eagle in flight, a' flyin' above the lake, was first of all a sign that Jeremiah Johnson would be laid to rest in the rocks, somewhere on a rugged slope of white granite that spans the whole distance between Lone Pine Lake and Mirror Lake— about a mile and a half.

He then told Cameron that he had put Jeremiah there himself, three years earlier, some 40 years after Cameron, as a boy, had seen the eagle in his dreams. Now, all this is what the grandson of Cameron White Eagle told me. His grandfather had told him these things. And there's more. He said that John Windwalker road off after he give his grandfather that letter, and no one ever saw him again—except one man, and I'll get to that…

It turns out that the letter contained a map—a detailed map of the actual restin' place of Jeremiah Johnson. When Windwalker showed him the map, he told White Eagle somethin' that was a mite strange. He said that when Johnson was an old man, he had asked him one day, in the harsh winter of 1927, to accompany him to Mirror Lake. Windwalker never

144

questioned Jeremiah; he just rode on up there with the ol' timer. Of course they were both old men, but Jeremiah's strength was fadin' fast—it was just his time.

They left their horses at Lone Pine Lake and climbed the granite slope just north of it on foot. They reached a place near a formation, where three pointed rocks of white granite stood above all the others. Just beyond those crags stood a shiny, black rock—a huge boulder of black volcanic glass, strange to that particular location. Volcanic deposits were not known to be there among the high arrays of granite.

Jeremiah stopped at the base of this boulder and then turned to face John Windwalker. He put forth a hand and told him that it was his place to die, and that he would 'lie down here.' He said to Windwalker that he must 'turn away and not look back.' He told him not to come back to this place for a time, which time would eventually be made known to him. He asked Windwalker to please do as he had asked.

John Windwalker put his hand forward and shook the hand of Jeremiah Johnson. He looked into his tearful eyes and told him, 'I will do as my great brother has asked of me. We shall walk in eternity together, my friend. I will now turn and walk away, again, as you have asked of me, though my heart is exceedingly grieved—good-bye, my good friend.'

John Windwalker climbed down that slope of granite, movin' a mite slow, but soon reached the horses. He rode down the mountain with Jeremiah's mount in tow, but he never looked back the whole time—kept his word. He returned to the ranch and continued his duties there. He told the others where Jeremiah was, but asked them not to visit the site. As far as White Eagle's grandson knew, only his grandfather had visited the site, and that was in 1930.

Windwalker told him to go up there three days after the Harvest Moon had faded from the sky. He gave White Eagle the letter and the map and told him that he had to fulfill his destiny. Again he mentioned that he would be the 'keeper of the Johnson legend,' but did not elaborate? Not long after that meetin', Windwalker disappeared and, as I said earlier, was not seen again in the High Sierra he so loved—not by any white man …

John Perez said that later that year, three days after the Harvest Moon had completed its cycle, his grandfather went up into the Whitney area. He rode up the ol', hiker's trail to Lone Pine Lake, where he dismounted. Now a' foot and usin' the somewhat worn and faded map as a guide, he stumbled upon the remains of a man that was lyin' on a platform made of leather-laced lodge pole pine, which rested atop a scaffold of the same construction. The man was covered with animal skins.

As he looked up toward the body, squintin' against the sunlight in his eyes, he suddenly heard the wings of a great bird on the wind. He kept the sun from his eyes best he could with a raised hand, that he might get a look at the winged creature. And so he did—it was a great white eagle! It soared above him majestically and right away began to circle the granite slopes where he stood.

As the great bird continued to circle above him, White Eagle climbed up the scaffold and peered under the animal skins. The man under cover had not been there long. It was John Windwalker, lyin' on his back and facin' the sky, who in life had given him the letter and map only three months earlier. Windwalker appeared to have died a natural death—perhaps of old age?

Naturally at this point I asked John Perez, 'What happened after your grandfather made that discovery?' Well, he said that Windwalker had a piece of leather in his hands—rolled up— like a scroll is kept. Both hands were on the scroll as it lay on the man's stomach. White Eagle's curiosity got the best of him, and so he carefully removed the scroll from Windwalker's

146

grasp. Just as that scroll come out of the dead man's hands that big eagle circlin' overhead screeched out all of a sudden like, its shrill breakin' the stillness of the high country and echoin' for a time along the face of that white granite mountain.

Well, that ear-rendin' 'screech' and the echo that followed scared the livin' daylights out of White Eagle. He climbed back down that scaffold in a big hurry—dang near fell, I was told. Once he was on the ground he looked up in the air again for that eagle, but couldn't see it nowhere in the sky—looked for it in earnest, too. He scratched at his head a little in wonder, then walked over and sat on a nearby granite boulder, where he tried to settle down a bit before he commenced to open up that leather scroll.

When he finally did get to unrollin' it, the first thing he noticed was *his name* written in at the top of the scroll, above a handwritten block of words. It was written afresh, much more recently than the somewhat faded printin' on the main body of the scroll. Just above that main body of writin', and below White Eagle's name, the document contained the near faded words, 'To my friend, John Windwalker.'

He looked up at Windwalker on the scaffold, then back at the scroll. He knew at that moment that he was meant to find the scroll, and meant to see this restin' place of Windwalker. 'Perhaps there is more,' he thought. This is what it read:

And God blessed those outlaws who rode off from the cave. The star of Bethlehem was in the sky that night. And the spirit of forgiveness was in the hearts of all men. I was allowed to be a part of this wondrous thing, and have been granted something that few men of dust are granted.

John Windwalker, you have been my closest friend for most of my life. When I am about to die, I will take you to the black rock, the volcanic glass that lies on the ridge below Mirror Lake. I shall lie down at the base of the rock and you shall walk away. Do not look back, for the Spirit of God will overshadow me in glory, and I shall go with Him into heaven before the time when all men shall see Him.

You yourself will not die until the appointed time. When the moon of the harvest approaches, three years from now, you will come back here to die. I will be here to greet your spirit, as I have been granted my request that you too can come to a wondrous place before the appointed time of men. You will find this scroll at the base of the great black rock where you left me.

Build a scaffold of lodge pole pine here and lie upon it. Hold this scroll in your hands when you lie down to die, and I will come. We will be together again in a land where there is no death. There will be great mountains, rimmed with tall pine, and crystal waters will flow through them. All the things we love will be there—the horses, the critters of the wild, and the majestic birds, and someday, all those people whom we loved in this life.

Your body of the earth will remain for a time as you have lain, so that those who see it, if any are allowed to do so, will not desecrate this place. It is hallowed ground, and it was here that my dream was allowed to come true. It is here that your dream will come true as well. I have not yet been told, but I feel most strongly that there are others whose dreams will come true here. We will know these people.[1]

Your friend, Jeremiah Johnson.

The letter, the map, and the scroll are now in the possession of White Eagle's grandson, John Perez, placed in his hands by his dyin' grandfather, in 2007. The old fella' was near a hundred-sixteen years old! He died at a nursing home in Bishop, California, just north of Big Pine. Perez said he was compelled to find me because I was the last livin' relative of

148

Jeremiah Johnson. He said he'd been tryin' to track me down for near two years—ever since his granddad had passed on.

He said that White Eagle told him that when he found me, he was to 'summon' me (that's the word he used) to gather a handful of soil from the restin' places of each of my parents. I was to put those samples in an airtight container and bring them from Ohio, in person, and meet with Running Horse in Arizona. I'm not sure I understand that request, but there's a reason for everything, and there are for sure things hard to understand in this entire matter.

John Perez believes that the scroll has great power. He wants me to go to the High Sierras with him—to the place marked on the map at Mirror Lake. He says it's my destiny—my family's destiny. I got a feelin' about this whole thing, and I'll get to that in a few minutes, but, you know what? I am goin'! Wild mustangs couldn't keep me away. I'm gonna' meet Running Horse in Tucson, and we're gonna' head for the high lonesome, you can count on that!

I wanted to tell this story so that those who read it will know what really happened to the legendary Jeremiah Johnson —a man who grabbed hold of life's meanin'. I wanted to tell it before I lit out and headed for the High Sierra myself. I probably won't ever be back, and no one will know where I am —no one will know the truth or be able to figure out where I might be and why I might be there, except perhaps those of you who have read this story.

What will you do with this story? You don't have the map, but you know *about* where the site is. If not, then know that Mirror Lake is on most topographical maps. You can find it. It's only about four and a half miles up from the Whitney Portal—just a mile and a half up past Lone Pine Lake. Somewhere in between and off the main trail is that shiny black rock—and maybe what's left of a lodge pole pine scaffold. Do you know what black volcanic glass looks like?

149

If you want to see a picture of this area, the picture you see just before chapter 1 of this writin' (page 14) was taken on the trail overlookin' Mirror Lake. The lake is just about in the center of the picture. Just over the back edge of the lake, as you're lookin' at it, between the white granite buttes and toward the Owens Valley, the trail drops onto a considerable stretch of granite (not visible in the picture) that descends a mile and a half to Lone Pine Lake. That black volcanic rock is somewhere in that maze of white granite—look for three sharp crags (tall, pointed rocks) close together—when and if you get there!

I have just a little more to say before I end this story and head West. After White Eagle read the scroll, he got up from that rock where he was a' sittin', and walked toward the scaffold. John Perez told me his granddad was lookin' down at the ground, thinkin' about the loss of his friend up there on that platform. When he got near the scaffold, which was built directly in front of that black rock, he saw somethin' he wasn't expectin'.

The rocks under the scaffoldin' were a mixture of stone size granite and shale—white and gray rock. He saw a couple bones a' lyin' there among the mix. As he begin to pay closer attention, he saw a human ribcage—about half covered by the stones and shale. He figured it couldn't be Johnson, because Windwalker had not buried him—he'd said his good-bye's to him at the black rock, some three feet away from where the scaffold stood. No one had put Jeremiah in the ground!

The bones didn't belong to Windwalker—he was up on the scaffold, and had just recently built the scaffold and climbed up on it to die. He must have seen the bones! He built the scaffold right over top of 'em! White Eagle then started pickin' at the stones and shale and movin' them aside.

He said he uncovered a complete skeleton before long, but found no clothin' or any other thing that might help him to identify the person—except a leather gunbelt, which was fastened around the waist of the remains—an ol' rusted pistol was in the holster—. 45 caliber, White Eagle said.

Animals could have torn the clothin' away—dragged it off or somethin', but this gunbelt was tough leather, and as I said, it was fastened around the skeleton's waist—fastened by a broad, sliver buckle. The face of the buckle bore a set of stamped letters on it; 'E' 'S'. White Eagle told his grandson that he didn't recollect anybody with them initials.

John Perez said his granddad left the gunbelt and the old rusted iron where it was. Said he kept the scroll, the letter, and the map, so that he could pass them on to Johnson's kin. Perez told me that the items were waitin' for me at his place in Tucson. When I got off the phone with him that day, I got to thinkin'—about them initials on that belt buckle. I told you at the very beginnin' of this story that I wasn't no dang fool. I can put things together pretty good when I really think about 'em.

Everyone thought that Ed Shay road off to Yosemite and was never heard from again. 'E' 'S'—I figure we *did* hear from Ed Shay. He may have rode off to Yosemite for a time, but that ain't where he ended up. Why did he go there? How did he know exactly where to go? And, who in thunder covered him up with rocks? Like I said earlier, I got a feelin' about this whole thing.

That feelin' is so profound that I dare not say anything about it to anyone at this particular time. I wish I was bold enough to tell you just what it is that I'm thinkin', but for some reason, I can't. It's beyond me, so to speak. I'm held back from doin' that.

Does that seem weird? Maybe I don't have to do it at all— or, maybe I'm not supposed to tell anyone. Life is strange. Things happen and thoughts jump in and swim around in your head that you just can't put into words—at least for a while, and maybe never.

It's said that the West was built on legends—tall tales that help us make sense of things too exceptional or strange to comprehend, and that legends are a way of understandin' things greater than ourselves—forces that shape our lives, events that defy explanation, and individuals whose lives soar to the heavens or fall to the earth. This is how legends are born.

I figure this whole story is much more than a legend—it's a distinct ray of hope—a most welcome light in a vastly darkened world—don't you?

THE END...

Of the story? I'd say, 'not hardly.' Thanks for listenin'. In a few days I'll be with Runnin' Horse (John Perez) in Tucson. We'll be headin' into the Sierras. I think we just might find somethin'—or some place—that dang few of us ever get to see. I figure a man's never too old to chase a dream—goes for the women too. Sometimes you have to believe in what you wish. An old song of the trail says it all…

Now the wind blows lonely, And you can't help thinkin',
Of the things that you're leavin' behind.
But you've got to gamble, On each new horizon,
When a dream's at the end of the line…
Ride boldly, ride!

I almost forgot—if there's any way I'm able to do it—if my wish comes true and I no longer need it, I'll just leave that scroll there for you, dear reader—at the base of the black rock. Running Horse says it has great power. You'll just have to ride boldly, ride! Adios.

In memory of John Milton Brandt 1945-2009

A High Sierra Christmas

References and Notes

From the Author
1. NASB, Jeremiah 17:9: *The heart is more deceitful than all else, and is desperately sick; Who can understand it?* Also, Matthew 19:17, Mark 7:21, John 15:5, Romans 7:18

Chapter 1
1. Just West of Lone Pine, the towering granite crest of the Sierra Nevada is one of the most majestic sights in California. Mt. Whitney crowns the escarpment; its 14,497-foot summit is the highest peak in the contiguous United States. It has been the mountain backdrop for many motion pictures filmed in the area for over six decades. Three local fishermen made the first *recorded* climb to this elusive summit from Lone Pine on August 18, 1873. The author of this book has climbed to the summit twice—September 1970, August 1998.

Chapter 2
1. NASB, John 1:3: *All things came into being by Him, and apart from Him nothing came into being that has come into being.* Also; Genesis 1:1, Exodus 20:11, Nehemiah 9:6, Job 12:7-10, Psalm 102:25, 104:5, Isaiah 40:28, 45:12, 48:13, Acts 4:24, 7:50, 14:15, 17:24, 1st Corinthians 8:6, Ephesians 3:9, Colossians 1:6, Hebrews 1:1,2, & 11:3.

Chapter 5
1. NASB, Romans 8:28: *And we know that God causes all things to work together for good to those who love God, to those who are called according to His purpose.*

Chapter 7
1. Our struggle with human nature is thoroughly explained by the Apostle Paul: NASB, Romans 7:14-24: *For we know that the Law is spiritual; bit I am of flesh, sold into bondage to sin. For that which I am doing, I do not understand; for I am not practicing what I would like to do, but I am doing the very thing I hate. But if I do the very thing I do not wish to do, I agree with the Law, confessing that it is*

155

good. So now, no longer am I the one doing it, but sin, which indwells me. For I know that nothing good dwells in me, that is, in my flesh; for the wishing is present with me, but the doing of the good is not. For the good that I wish, I do not do; but I practice the very evil that I do not wish. But if I am doing the very thing I do not wish, I am no longer the one doing it, but sin, which dwells in me. I find then the principle that evil is present with me, the one who wishes to do good. For I joyfully concur with the Law of God in the inner man, but I see a different law in the members of my body, waging war against the law of my mind, and making me a prisoner of the law of sin, which is in my members. Wretched man that I am! Who will free me from the body of this death?

2. Nature and all of its inhabitants are to be our teachers. We are instructed to learn from them: NASB, Job 12: 7-10: *But now ask the beasts, and let them teach you; and the birds of heaven, and let them tell you. Or speak to the earth, and let it teach you; and let the fish of the sea declare to you. Who among all these does not know that the hand of the Lord has done this, in whose hand is the life of every living thing, and the breath of all mankind?*

3. The whole world is guilty before God. No one is excused. Therefore, one needs to examine his/her self. In whatever way you might deal with others, you will be dealt with in the same way yourself, for all have sinned. Also, you will need to become perfect before you seek to correct anyone else, and that will never happen (your perfection) in this lifetime. Matthew 7:1-3: *Do not judge lest you be judged. For in the way you judge, you will be judged; and by your standard of measure, it will be measured to you. And why do you look at the speck that is in your brothers eye, but do not notice the log that is in your own eye?* Also, Mark 4:24, Luke 6:36-38.

4. NASB, 1st Corinthians 3:18-21: *Let no man deceive himself. If any man among you thinks he is wise in this age, let him become foolish that he may become wise. For the wisdom of this world is foolishness before God. For it is written, 'He is the One who catches the wise in their craftiness,' and again, 'The Lord knows the reasoning's of the*

wise, that they are useless.' So then, let no one boast in men. Also, 1st Corinthians 1:25.

5. NASB, Galatians 3:22-28: *But the Scripture has shut up all men under sin, that the promise by faith in Jesus Christ might be given to those who believe. But before faith came, we were kept in custody under the law, being shut up to the faith, which was later to be revealed. Therefore the Law has become our tutor to lead us to Christ, that we may be justified by faith. But now that faith has come, we are no longer under a tutor. For you are all sons of God through faith in Christ Jesus. For all of you who were baptized into Christ have clothed yourselves with Christ. There is neither Jew nor Greek, there is neither slave nor free man, and there is neither male nor female; for you are all one in Christ Jesus.*

Chapter 8

1. *Angel's Flight*:

Angel's Flight is a real place, and looks exactly as it's described in the story. Its actual location however is on the Eastern Sierra's Carson Peak Trail, just west of Silver Lake on the June Lake loop. The trail to the Flight's base leaves Silver Lake via Gem Pass. The Flight is on the last section of that trail as you approach Gem Lake, about three miles from the trailhead at Silver Lake. Once atop the Flight, the trail continues on through the Ansel Adams Wilderness and on into Yosemite through Tuolumne Meadows.

The author both climbed and descended the Flight on horseback in 1987, with fellow police officers Ron Bailey, Al LaFlame, and Al Edler, along with Jim Coates, owner of a local motel in the Silver Lake area. After the climb, the riders continued about fifteen miles back into the wilderness and camped for a week. They spent time fishing the high lakes, exploring the rugged wilderness, and made the ascent to Lost Lakes, a remote fishing spot, surrounded by several lofty crags that appear from a distance as the jaw and sharp-pointed teeth of a giant dragon.

On the return trip, the descent down Angel's Flight was after sunset. The winds blew and the sparks off the horse's hooves flew, but everyone made it down in one piece. Jim Coates had experienced

157

the Flight many times when it was covered in ice. His animal had never broke stride during those encounters, and he never lost a pack mule. There's a pack station at Silver Lake, where you can rent horses, pack mules and wranglers, who act as guides for the trip up Angel's Flight.

You can ride as far as you want to and as long as you want to on the trail. If you're camping, you can ride up to your campsite—the wranglers will pack up your gear for the ride up, unpack your gear at your chosen campsite, take the horses and mules back down, and come back with the same to pack you up when you're ready to leave. It's a fine vacation for anyone who wants to experience life on the trail the old way. The pack station also offers guides for hunting trips on horseback. Some packages include meals and camping gear, if you cannot bring your own.

2. Water Baptism; Acts 2:37,38, & Romans 6:1-11

3. Sharing and caring, NASB, *Acts 2:44, 4:32-35*

Chapter 9
1. The Christmas Story, NASB, *Matthew 1:18 thru 2:12, Luke 1:1 thru 2:20, John 1:1-5, and John 1:14*

2. The tongue, NASB, *James 3:1-12*

Epilogue
1. What really happens after death?

I believe that only the dead can answer that particular question. The Bible does speak of many who were seen alive after death. They are as follows: Samuel (*1ˢᵗ Samuel 28:11-19*), Moses (*Matthew 17:3, Mark 9:4—note here that Elijah was with Moses, however, Elijah had never known death*), Lazarus (*John 11:44, 12:1,2*), and many deceased saints, who came out of their tombs in Jerusalem, just after Jesus' resurrection, and who also appeared to many people in the city (*Matthew 27:51-53*).

The Bible records two men who entered heaven having never seen physical death. These were Enoch (*Geneses 5:24, Hebrews*

158

11:5), and Elijah (*2nd Kings 2:1-12*). If there were others, God chose not to reveal their names in the Scriptures, which stands firm as His only written revelation to us.

All things are possible to those who believe (*Mark 9:23*). However, we must consider all things that happen in our lives (or that happen in other people's lives, or things that we hear about which fall into the category of paranormal) in the light of Scripture. If the Scriptures can verify as truth any of our concerns in any of these matters, then we can be on solid ground in our beliefs in those matters; no matter how unbelievable or strange they might seem to us.

It is my personal belief, as a teacher of God's truth, that life after death and the presence of spirits in our world is most possible. We also must keep in mind that the world itself is under the dominion of deceitful, evil rulers from the *spiritual realms* (*Ephesians 6:12*). With everything that's happening in our world today, we would be more than wise to take this fact into consideration—in everything that we might think, and in every action that we might take as a result of our thinking.

Finally, all who are now in their graves *will come forth* in the resurrection, when Christ returns. The sea will also give up its dead. Those who are found in Christ (true believers), whether alive or dead at the time, will be 'changed.' In the twinkling of an eye, their bodies of corruption and mortality will put on incorruption and immortality. Evil and death will be destroyed, and we can look forward to new heavens and a new earth, where only goodness dwells—forever.
(1st Corinthians 15, all, 1st Thessalonians 4:13-18, 2nd Peter 3:7-13, Revelation 20:12,13)

A HIGH SIERRA CHRISTMAS
An Untold Tale of Jeremiah Johnson
(Latest Holiday Edition July 2010)

From
LONE WOLF LIMITED
A Division of
M S Taylor Productions
1997-2010

LaVergne, TN USA
16 December 2010

209003LV00004B/25/P

[13]